Outlaw Heartstrings

MariaLisa deMora

First Published 2025

ISBN 13: 978-1-946738-82-0

DEDICATION

Well I'm going, with or without you.
~ Brave Little Toaster

For me, the one who never thought this could happen
to begin with, much less a reboot. <finger guns>
Proved ya wrong!.

Contents

ACKNOWLEDGMENTS

Welp, I'm back, sorta.

There are few things more humbling than running straight into the fraility of ones own body. After a year and a half, I'm not really back, no matter how much I want it to be true.

Between the various and many falls, surgeries, illnesses, concussion/TBI, and broken bones, 2023 and 2024 are my years to forget.

Because of <gestures vaguely> all that, and the residual effects of the TBI, it meant working on this story was two steps forward, five steps back. But we persevered, me and Irish and Ellen, because this tale may have started as a short story in an anthology, but it has been brought to life as a novella one hard-fought sentence at a time.

And here we all are, the three of us, hoping that readers love the story and characters. Not gonna lie, there's more nervousness now than with the first ever book, because I never thought anyone would see that one. This one, I halfway hope people read it and I halfway hope they don't. No, I wholeway hope they do!

This novella was first published in the anthology *12 Bikers for Christmas*, way back in 2022. It's been modified, with quite a lot of new content added. If you read it back then, and still bought this copy, I'm deeply grateful for your trust and love.

Woofully yours,
~ML

Outlaw Heartstrings

Liam "Irish" Connor and his ride-or-die brother Lyon Baxter lived for the roar of their bikes and the freedom of the road as members of the Liars & Fools Motorcycle Club. Bound by loyalty thicker than blood, the two men shared a life of wild rides and wilder nights—until a deadly ambush shattered their world, leaving Irish kneeling in the dirt, his brother's blood on his hands.

Haunted by Lyon's death, Irish sets out on a pilgrimage to Bozeman, Montana, to pay his respects at his brother's grave. But the road has other plans. A blown tire strands him in the small Wyoming town of Grass Creek, where fate introduces him to Ellen, a widow with a spark that reignites his soul, and her spirited daughter, Lucy. As Irish finds himself drawn into the warmth of a new community, and the arms of a woman who understands his pain, he faces a choice: cling to the ghosts of his past or embrace a future that feels like home.

Before the Road

The North Carolina hills rolled out like a crumpled blanket under the late summer sun, heat shimmering off the asphalt where Liam Connor straddled his bike. The engine growled beneath him, a steady heartbeat syncing with his own, loping along contentedly. Next to him, Lyon Baxter leaned over his own ride, fiddling with a carburetor that'd been giving him hell all week. His grease-streaked hands moved with the confidence of a man who'd been born to wrench, and his crooked and wild grin flashed up at Liam.

"Why so glum, Irish? Give me just a couple more minutes. Fuckin' thing's gonna purr like a kitten by the time I'm done," Lyon said, wiping sweat from his brow with the back of his wrist. "Then we're ridin' to the coast, brother. Big helpings of beer, sand, and women. Big. Large helpings. We'll run the fortune in that order to start, then turn it around and find more women. Riding to the coast with your brother. Best way to spend a weekend."

Irish chuckled. He killed the bike's engine and put down the kickstand. Still sitting on the bike, he rolled a pebble with the toe of his boot. "You say that every time, Ly. Last trip, you spent half the night pukin' up cheap whiskey and the other half cryin' about that redhead who wouldn't give you her number."

"Details, man. Details." Lyon's laugh was a bark, sharp and bright, cutting through the humid air. "Point is, we ride together. Always do."

That was the truth of it. Lyon had been Irish's shadow since they were kids tearing through the backwoods on beat-up dirt bikes, joined the military together, and then once discharged, patched into the Liars & Fools MC within a month of each other. Lyon was the loud one, the reckless one, the one who'd jump off a bridge just to see if the water was deep enough. Irish was the steady hand, the one who pulled him back—or jumped in after him when he couldn't be stopped. Brothers, not by blood, but by something thicker.

The day Lyon died, that thickness turned to tar. It was a run gone wrong. So fucking wrong. They'd been ambushed by a rival club out on a lonely stretch of highway. Bullets flew, and Lyon took one to the chest, falling immediately. In moments Irish's hands were slick with his brother's blood. He ignored the still raging battle as he tried to hold life inside a body that wouldn't keep it. "Stay with me, Ly," he'd begged, voice cracking like a boy's. "Hold on, brother." But Lyon's grin faded, his eyes went dull, and Irish was left kneeling in the dirt, a hole in his soul where his brother used to be.

After Lyon's death, the club tried to stitch itself back together, but Irish couldn't. Every ride felt like a ghost was tailing him, every laugh a betrayal of the silence Lyon left behind. His vest hung heavier, the Liars & Fools patch a weight he wasn't sure how long he could still carry.

Then came a final and unexpected letter from Lyon's mother. He'd been haunting her phone a couple times a week since Ly passed. The woman was a haughty bitch, and she was in fine form with this final letter. The delivery of the requested details was cold as ever, curtly conveying she'd had Lyon's ashes buried in Bozeman. *Fucking Bozeman. In fucking Montana. Snow and cold nine months out of the year. Wouldn't have been Ly's choice of final resting places.* There'd been no invite to whatever limited services she'd had for Ly, which hadn't given Irish a chance to say a final goodbye, just the curt note. He knew it probably pissed her off to even include an address. She'd always hated Ly's life in the club, her only boy, riding the wind far outside of her controlling efforts. And she'd always blamed Irish.

Irish stared at that letter for the hundredth time over the weeks, the paper creasing under his fingers. He didn't owe her shit, but he owed Lyon everything. So, he packed his bags, fueled up Hester, and hit the road. A promise to his brother, a pilgrimage to lay the demons to rest. He didn't know what he'd find out there. Alone. Closure, maybe, or just more ghosts. But the highway called, and Irish answered, the wind in his ears drowning out the echo of Lyon's last laugh.

Roadside Assistance

Irish

"Sonufa…"

Liam Connor, also known as Irish, braked and cautiously steered the bike towards the narrow shoulder of the small Wyoming county highway, glad to see it wasn't too steeply sloped, at least. The racketing thuds bouncing the bike underneath his ass were in counterpoint to the thumping of his racing heart. Nothing like a blowout at highway speeds to get the adrenaline flowing.

Once safely on the side of the road, he took a moment to balance the bike between his thighs, noting the way his body trembled.

"Just watch...next, it'll be no cell service," he grumbled as he thumbed the kill switch and heeled down the kickstand.

This entire trip had seemed fraught with issues. Between pop-up rainstorms and a tank of bad gas, he wasn't as close to his destination as he'd planned. Longer routes chosen had something to do with it, but he'd found the closer he drew to Bozeman, the easier it was to take another break or chase twisty curves. Now with a blown back tire? At minimum, he was looking at a wrecker and a shop visit before he'd be able to get back on the road.

Eyeing the dark clouds scudding along the horizon, Irish wondered if snow might be the next hurdle.

He'd known making this trip so close to Christmas would be a crapshoot on weather conditions, but he wasn't going back on his promise of making this trip before New Year. This one would mark two years without Lyon.

"No backing out now. Not if I can help it." *Hooah.*

Swinging off the bike, he studied the sloping angle it leaned on the stand and shook his head. The back tire was shredded, and turning to look back the way he'd come showed the lane littered with bits of rubber.

At least it was the rear. Coulda been worse.

Irish yanked his phone from the front pocket of his vest and unlocked it, glaring at the words replacing the normal bars.

"Called it."

He tried to remember the name of the last town he'd rolled through. *Masters or Anders or something like that*, he thought. At least twenty minutes ago, which meant more than twenty miles in his rearview. *Hell of a long way to hoof it.* A quick dig into his side bag surfaced the compact atlas he always carried, a holdover from before smartphones. Bending and folding the pages, he homed in on the area where he stood. *Probably*. Within thirty miles or so. *Give or take a handful of miles.*

Based on the timeline in his head, the closest town of any size on the map was about ten miles ahead. An extended walk for the few remaining hours of daylight. "Won't be the first forced nighttime hike," he muttered, refolding the map. "Just gotta plan ahead."

Water bottle in hand, he pocketed the bike's key and gave the tank a pat. "Be back soon, girl."

He'd made it about a mile up the road when he heard the rumble of a truck engine. Glancing over his shoulder back in the direction he'd come, Irish saw an older pickup already slowing down and pulling to the shoulder. The driver was a hulking shadow figure, easily taking up half the cab.

Irish reversed direction and strode towards the truck as the driver door opened and the tallest man he'd ever seen poured out. The broad smile splitting an unkempt beard looked genuine, though, and his gut said this man wasn't a danger. *Yeah, like my gut's always right. Not.*

"Hey," he said with a smile and outstretched hand. "Liam Connor...Irish. Am I ever glad to see a friendly face on this stretch of road."

"Richard DeShed. Friends call me Ricky." The hand that clasped his was warm and dry, calloused fingers strong as they wrapped around his without hesitation. "That your bike back a ways?" Two pumps up and down and Richard "call me Ricky" released his grip to hook a thumb over his shoulder. "Looked like the tire blew on ya."

"Yeah, was a wild ride for half a heartbeat. She's never let me down, though, got me safe to the side of the road. You know a wrecker service around here that loads bikes? My phone's got no service, so I couldn't search or call anyone."

"This stretch of the road is too far between towers. There's like a fifteen-mile stretch that goes by fast if you're rollin', but probably feels like a bitchslap from the universe when you're needing help." Ricky tipped his head towards the truck. "Climb in. I got folks we can get to help. Where ya headed?"

By the time Irish had opened the passenger door, Ricky was already sprawled in the seat behind the steering wheel. He'd unhooked a microphone from underneath the dash and was fiddling with dials on the front of a familiar black box.

"CB radio, huh? Guess that makes sense out here." Out of habit, Irish removed his vest and folded it to drape across a knee as he took a seat on the bench seat. "Not really something that works on a bike."

That earned him another beard-splitting grin. "My ole lady thinks I'm nuts for holding on to this dinosaur, but she'll be singing a different tune tonight." He clicked the button on the mic. "Dechamps, you on this channel, bud?" He released the button for a beat, and the static from the speakers filled the space between them. Another soft click, then, "Champ, get your ass off the can and get on the radio. Got a job for you, man."

More static, and then a voice sounding far away spoke. "Is that Sir Sheds a Lot? Man, I wouldn't get off the can for you. Good thing I'm standing in the office, then, isn't it? What ya need?"

"Bike on the side of the road out past the Neals. Shredded back tire. Bring your ramps and straps, man. Let's get this loaded up." Ricky pulled his leg into the truck and slammed the door. "We're up the road a couple miles, but I'll beat you back to it. We'll wait."

"What kind of bike? Little one, we can just lift it up won't need nothin' special. Talk to me." Dechamps's question didn't keep Ricky from starting the truck and wheeling them in a U-turn.

"Bring the ramps, man. Cruiser, so probably a grand and change when it comes to the weight." Ricky glanced at Irish, who nodded; that was a good estimate if the bike was full of fuel. Ricky keyed the mic again and asked, "ETA?"

"Give me ten minutes to gather everything, then another fifteen for the drive. See you soon."

"Ask him if he takes credit." Irish didn't have the kind of cash on him for a wrecker bill. "And if he knows a shop he can take the bike to that'll have a back tire."

"Irish here wants to know if you take credit, Champ. We'll be taking the bike to Dolph's shop. Call him before you get out of town, let him know what we're doin'."

"I'll call Dolph now. Reassure your boy. Yeah, I take credit. I take chickens in trade sometimes, too, so credit is cool." Dechamps's voice was filled with amusement, evident even over the tinny speaker for the radio. "Cool is good."

"See you in a few. Out." Ricky offered Irish another wide smile as they rolled up the highway. "Sorted. If Dolph don't have the right kind of tire, we'll figure that out too." He reached down and tweaked one of the knobs on the radio, then lifted the mic again. "Momma, you got your ears on?" The button unclicked. "Told you she thinks this is ridiculous. She's gonna eat those words tonight. We need the radio since we're stuck on this stretch of the highway for a bit." He lifted the mic to his mouth. "Momma, gimme some lovin'. This is your Ricky Dicky giving you a ringy dingy." The hand holding the mic dropped to his thigh. "She loves that shit. Silly talkin' makes her happy."

The radio clattered, and another burst of static came over the speakers, then a melodic female voice. "Mr. Ricky, Ms. Marilyn says to cut that out on the public radio."

"Told ya, she loves it." He lifted the mic, the coiled wire stretching. "Ellen, darlin', tell Momma I'm in need of her dulcet tones." Tongue out, Ricky laughed. "Ellen's our daughter-in-law. She won't pass on the specific message, but guarantee you Momma's in hearing range anyway. She gonna try and give me some shit, you just watch."

There was a longer pause, then the radio crackled loudly. "Richard Trinity DeShed, you need to stop this nonsense now." This voice was deeper, older, and the speaker clearly exasperated. "I'll talk to you when you get home, you old codger."

"Loves it. Told ya." They'd gotten to where the bike was parked, and Ricky effortlessly swung wide in another U-turn to pull in behind Irish's bike. He keyed the mic with a laugh. "Momma, I'm bringing home a wandering soul. Set another place for supper, would ya?"

"Lord, Ricky, why didn't you lead with that? Who is it? Hi, stranger, I forget sometimes the CB has no privacy. You're welcome here, of course."

"His name is Liam Connor, and he had a blowout on his bike. Man's lucky to be alive. Probably need some cherry pie to help settle his nerves." Ricky gave Irish a grin and a wink. "Poor fella's phone won't work out here, so I found him walking up the road. He's plum give out, Momma."

"And pie is a salve for all ills, I know. I'll be ready. You know we've always got extra in the pot. You've a good heart, Ricky."

"I try, Momma. Love you bunches, woman. Out." Ricky pointed up the road. "Think I see Champs headin' this way. We'll get things buttoned up and then head home. You need to get anything from the bike? Dolph's shop's secure. He's got cameras inside and out, but it's late for him to work on it tonight. You'll bunk up at my house, and we'll head over first thing in the morning."

"Tomorrow's Christmas Eve. You think he'll be open? Maybe I should get Dechamps to take the bike to another shop?" Tightness in Irish's chest needed a hard breath to break through. "Folks don't want strangers around on holidays, man. I can sleep next to the bike. Wouldn't be the first time. It's why I've got a bedroll."

"Oh, yeah. Grass Creek's not too big, but Dolph'll get you rollin' again sooner than a larger shop. Champ takin' the bike to the next town wouldn't be a problem, but you'd have to go all the way to Cody to get to another shop. Next town won't help you none." Ricky unfastened his seat belt and slouched against the door. "As to sleepin' in the shop, Momma'd have my head if I let that happen. You won't be any trouble, and she digs helpin' out. We've got a guest room I guarantee she's airing out right now, probably changing the sheets."

"If you're sure it's no trouble." The wavering illusion Ricky had pointed out on the horizon evolved into the shape of a decent-sized wrecker. "I'd be obliged. I can pay."

"No need. The room would go unused otherwise, and my ole lady wasn't kidding when she said there's always extra food in the pot. Woman don't know how to cook small, which was a blessing when we were raising our boy, but now that it's just a handful of us, means lots of days of leftovers." Ricky straightened his oversized frame, leaning towards the door as his fingers curled around the handle. "It'll be a blessing to me, you eatin' some of whatever she's got cooked for supper. Excellent in the kitchen, but there's only so many days a man can stand the same meal on a plate."

Irish grinned and slipped out of the truck on his side, meeting Ricky at the front of the vehicle. Seemed like the stories of western rural hospitality weren't stories at all, but reality. The openness and willingness to help were in contradiction to where he'd grown up, and already he knew which he liked better. They stood and waited as the wrecker worked through a three-point turn, angling back towards the bike until Irish grew a little nervous of the proximity, but the vehicle stopped with a solid yard of distance between the back of the bed and the bike.

"Not his first time. He'll take care of your girl." Ricky's hand landed on Irish's shoulder in a surprise grip that felt oddly reminiscent of one his brothers back home delivered often.

Brothers. Strange how he hadn't thought of them too much on this whole trip. *Too focused on the end goal.* Which meant he also hadn't been really present as he'd rolled through Wyoming, featuring some of the prettiest vistas in the country. He didn't remember running over anything that would have damaged the tire, and didn't remember any tell-tale bulges in the sidewalls, but if he were honest with himself, either could have happened and he might not have registered it.

"Irish." He extended his hand towards the man who'd exited the cab of the wrecker. Dechamps was the polar opposite of Ricky: short where Ricky was tall, broad versus a runner's build. He shook his head. "I appreciate you comin' all the way out here on my behalf."

"Hold that thought." Dechamps paused next to a row of controls and used them to adjust the angle of the truck bed, extending it by those few feet and then tipping until the edge of the metal kissed the asphalt of the shoulder. "Tow's a tow, but it's not often I get a chance to stretch my skills. Bikes are challenging, but probably the most fun I get to have legally." He grabbed a narrow ramp from the tool area behind the cab and notched one end into a slot in the bed before making his way to Irish. Dechamps's grip and handshake were strong without being overpowering. "I've had ample experience, though, with this old reprobate and his buddies. Least a coupla times a month he'll haul me out of bed for a roadside pickup for one of his club."

Irish spun to look at Ricky in a new light, surprised when the man sported an embarrassed grin. "You ride?"

"I might." He spread his hands wide with an exaggerated shrug. "Surprise?"

"No wonder you didn't flinch at picking me up." Irish approached him with a hand outstretched, gripping Ricky's thumb this time and folding their clenched fists between their chests as he pulled him in for a back-pounding clench. "Thanks, man."

It explained a lot. The references to ole lady and old man as Ricky and his wife sparred on the radio, the approving nod he'd given Irish when he'd folded his vest instead of wearing it inside a cage.

"Momma'd kill me if she knew I violated the code, man." Ricky chuckled, then sobered. "No room in my home for any beefs. Wanna throw that out there now, man. Legends MC is an open book, mostly, but just in case."

"My club is a small one, nestled down in the North Carolina hills. Doubt we'd have any issues, and I can guarantee you that I personally do not. You saw my vest. Are the Liars & Fools known to you?"

"Nope, not a bit. Which is why I didn't introduce myself sooner. Wasn't an issue." Ricky's shoulder lifted in an easy shrug as he turned to face Dechamps. "Better grab your bag and stuff before Champs gets her loaded up. Easier to get to now."

With a grunt, Irish moved and knelt next to the bike. He rummaged through the saddlebag that held his personals, the other side used for tools, oil, and other supplies needed for a long trip like this. He had a cheap gym bag strapped over the top of his bedroll, and it was the work of moments to release it. Ditty bag shoved inside, he stood and dug in his pocket, pulling out the small wad of keys. Irish stripped off the ring holding the keys for the bike and handed it over to Dechamps, who had walked closer.

"Where were you going?" Dechamps tied a tag to the keys before dropping them into his coat pocket, then wiggled the handlebars to ensure the forks weren't locked. Irish hadn't even thought to do that before he'd walked away from the bike earlier, much less lock the saddlebags. *Need to find my focus.* "Before you—" Dechamps leaned down and whistled low. "Had an epic blowout. There's hardly anything left of the tire, man. That had to be a thrill."

"You could call it that." Irish's laugh sounded more like a chainsaw than humor. "Bozeman. That's where I'm headed."

"Bozeman, huh?" Ricky stepped up beside Irish. "Got family up that way?"

Memories swamped Irish.

He gripped Lyon's hand tightly, blood making the hold tenuous, requiring Irish reseat their connection every few seconds. "Hold on, brother. Help's coming."

He watched as the light faded from his best friend's eyes, leaving them clouded and wrong. Life and the essence of what made Lyon leaking out of him sure as the red spilled to the highway.

He shook the visions off, those monsters that had haunted him for nearly a year, wishing for the familiar weight of his vest.

"Visiting a friend." The words sounded choked to his own ears.

Lyon's mother didn't even come to pick up the body, asking just for an urn to be shipped to her. That had bugged Irish, because at least Lyon had family. *Not everybody does. She should have done better by him.* It had taken Irish weeks to weasel the information out for where she'd laid the last part of Lyon to rest. This trip wasn't penance, but he'd hoped it would help lay to rest the demons that rode him so hard.

"You have a hard arrival date? We could get you a cage to take up if Christmas was the goal." Ricky made a face. "Gonna be snow tonight anyway. That alone will make riding through those hills between here and there chancy."

"No one's expecting me. Won't matter when I show up, except to me. I just wanted to be there before New Year's." That night would mark a full year since Lyon passed. It was the marker in Irish's life, things tidily divided into before and after categories. "So no rush if it does snow. I can get a motel."

"Nothing along those lines until Cody, kind of like the bike shop situation. I'm telling you, Marilyn will be pissed as hell at me if I don't bring you home now." Ricky pulled a grimace, then grinned to show he wasn't being too serious.

Dechamps laughed as he brought the bike upright, using the toe of a boot to lift the kickstand. "You do not want to piss off Marilyn. Better to just roll with it, Irish."

"Yeah, okay. Wouldn't want to be the reason Ricky here caught grief from Marilyn." Irish rolled his shoulders, again wishing for the familiar caress of leather. "Ready to load her up?" He slapped a hand against the seat. "She won't give you any trouble, promise. Hester's a good girl."

"Me and Hester are gonna get along just fine." It was a straight shot from where the bike sat to the ramp, and Dechamps started muscling the bike into place.

Irish and Ricky each leaned in, hands on the seat and frame as they shoved the bike upward. They paused and held it into place when the rear wheel had cleared the ramp, Dechamps making quick work of securing the straps Irish hadn't even noticed him spreading out. Kickstand down and heeled over, the bike looked odd on the sloped surface. He waited next to it as Dechamps jumped off the side and used the hydraulic controllers to bring the bed back to level, sliding it into place with a heavy metallic thump.

"Give Hester a good shake. See if you can move her at all." Irish did as asked, finding the bike was solidly strapped down. He suspected Dechamps's instructions had been to allay any fears he might have, and he appreciated the unspoken understanding.

"Good to go. Looks like." He made the jump off the bed, landing lightly next to Ricky, who offered him the bag retrieved from the shoulder. "Want help unloading at the bike shop?"

"Nah. Dolph's got two boys who still live at home. They'll treat her right."

"They better or Dodger'll have their asses." Ricky laughed. "Dolph's in Legends, too, and his boys are wanting to be second generation. He won't tolerate anything except respect for the machine, Irish. You got nothing to worry about there. He'll call once he gets an idea on the replacement tire, but we can head on home now."

"If you're sure, Dechamps?" Irish lifted a hand to the back of his neck, rubbing the tense muscles he hadn't noticed until moving the bike called out the stiffness. "You'll give Ricky a holler?"

"Sure thing." Dechamps stripped off his gloves and tossed them into the open door of the wrecker. "We can settle up when you come into town tomorrow to check on Hester."

Irish suppressed a smile. He liked the way the man had immediately taken to the name he used for the bike. It spoke to a familiarity with bikers in general, and that kind of understanding went a long way to alleviate any remaining unease at seeing his girl roped and tied down.

Following Ricky back to the truck, he unzipped the bag and tucked his vest inside. Not only wouldn't he wear it inside a cage, but it would be disrespectful to fly his colors inside another man's home unless they were part of the club or a close support group. Irish resigned himself to the unease that came from feeling naked without the leather riding his back.

They'd been underway for a few minutes, silence sitting comfortably between the two men when Ricky spoke up.

"Won't bother me none, you wear your cut in my home. Appreciate the clear respect you've got for your patch, brother."

Irish's head swung to look at Ricky, and he made a questioning sound.

"Serious as shit, Irish. You wearin' your cut won't bring you any grief in my home. From anyone." Ricky laughed softly. "And I suspect we'll have visitors once Dechamps explains to Dodger what's what. Momma knows the crew's ways, and no doubt she's already expecting it and will have plenty to feed everyone. You wearin' your cut is only right."

"I appreciate that." Irish's few words were heartfelt, and he took an easier breath. "Someone not in the life wouldn't get it. I shoulda known you'd be different."

Silence fell again, this time even more welcoming and comfort filled.

It seemed only minutes passed until Ricky steered the truck up a short lane ending in front of a large, sprawling house. The central windows of the residence were bright with flashing lights in the shape of a Christmas tree, and as they pulled up to a slowly opening garage door, more lights flashed on inside.

"Momma's gonna greet us." Ricky's words were filled with soft affection. "Woman's worth her weight in gold, and I try to never let her forget it."

Sure enough, the truck had barely rolled to a stop before the inside door burst open, and a tall woman swung down the couple of steps to the garage floor. She turned and scooped up a small child, propping what looked like a little girl on her hip as she rounded the front of the truck to the driver side. The woman was pretty, with a broad smile and bright blonde hair curling around her shoulders. The child was as different as day was to night, dark hair a long shaggy mess she still tried to hide behind when she saw Irish in the cab.

"That's my girls," Ricky boomed as he opened the door. "Momma, give me some sugar. Lucy girl, how are you, darlin'?"

Irish climbed out of the truck and put the bag back on the seat, unzipping to retrieve his cut. He'd just settled it on his shoulders when Ricky called his name.

"Irish, this is Marilyn, light of my life. And our granddaughter, Lucy, who puts the stars in our eyes every single day."

Irish looked up with a smile and a wave. "Ma'am, Lucy. Pleased to meetcha." A sound behind him pulled his attention back to the doorway in time to see a gorgeous dark-haired woman pause before skipping down the steps.

She had a ridged scar running along her jawline, but it didn't detract from her beauty at all.

Her bright green eyes danced with laughter as she held her arms out. "LouCiel, are you supposed to be outside this time of night?"

"I'm not o'side, momma. Me's i'side." Lucy pointed up. "Is woof. Me's i'side, no o'side." She hugged Marilyn's arm tighter. "Is MeMa brought me."

"Irish, this is Ellen, our daughter-in-love." Ricky's face flashed with an emotion for a moment that looked like sadness, then he brightened. "She's Lucy's ever-tolerant mother."

Irish tilted his head in acknowledgment, even as he tamped back the rich attraction swirling in his belly. Daughter-in-law meant entirely unavailable. Next through the door would be the son and husband, and there'd be hell to pay if anyone saw the way his dick had chubbed up in those few seconds. *Figures that the first time in a year I've been interested in someone would be here and now.*

"Welcome, Irish." Ellen's soft greeting didn't do anything for the state of his threatening erection. "Dinner's ready in a few, but we've got a room all setup for you to drop your things." She took Lucy from Marilyn's arms. "Follow me and the monster here and we'll show you."

"I not a m'nster." Lucy's complaint was broken with a big yawn.

"Lead the way, ma'am." Irish followed her slim form through the door into a narrow mudroom, entering a kitchen almost as large as Irish's entire apartment back home. Savory scents filled the space, and he sniffed in appreciation. "I appreciate your family taking me in like this. I was expecting a cold camp tonight."

"Oh goodness no, not if Ricky has any say about it. He and Marilyn are some of the most welcoming people I know." Ellen looked over her shoulder, dark hair falling down her back in a black flow. "I'm so lucky to have them in my life."

The hallway they traversed was lined with images on both sides. It appeared that Ricky and Marilyn had four sons, as the photos showed them in stuttering leaps of ages from clustered around their parents' legs to graduation and beyond. Three wedding photos included one of Ellen standing next to a tall, handsome man, his gaze fixed on her lovingly. Then a picture of the same man holding a tiny pink bundle, presumably Lucy. After that, the images of him ended, and it was just Ellen and Lucy, sometimes included with Ricky and Marilyn. *Wonder what happened.*

"Here's you." Ellen stepped past a doorway and motioned to the opening. "I'll leave you to get settled. It's got an attached bathroom, so you don't have to worry about sharing with anyone. We'll be putting plates down in twenty minutes or so, and you don't want to miss Marilyn's cooking." She offered a smile, and he liked how she held her head high, the scar on her face not seeming to be a consideration as she looked him in the eye. "Welcome, Irish."

"Liam." He instinctively wanted to hear what he considered his true name on her lips. "My friends call me Liam."

Her gaze flicked down to the name patch and back to his eyes. "Liam," she amended with a nod. "Welcome."

***

Ellen

As the man's government name rolled off her lips, Ellen knew she was in trouble. Not that she'd act on it, not under her in-law's roof, but the man in front of her ticked all the boxes on her holy-shit-he's-attractive list. Rough but gentlemanly, with a coarse voice paired with soft words—it was as if Irish...*Liam* had been created with her in mind.

For the first time in the years since the accident that had taken Jerry away, Ellen felt the stirring of physical attraction. She lowered her lashes, hoping to hide it from this man who seemed entirely too perceptive. She'd watched him registering the transition of images in the hallway; had marked the moment when he put together the weight of her loss.

LouCiel shifted on her hip, and Ellen grabbed hold of that distraction with an urgency that surprised her. "Sweet monster, let's get you settled so Mommy can eat supper with the grown-ups." Pressing a gentle kiss to her daughter's temple, she briefly met Liam's gaze. "She's already had dinner, and it's time for sleep. Just come back to the kitchen when you're ready. No rush." Noise traveled down the hallway, voices she recognized, and Ellen fought to hide a grimace. *Nick. Hope he minds himself this time.* The man kept fighting to get Ellen alone. He creeped her out with his protective attention. *He needs to find a woman.* "That'll be some of Ricky's boys. Sounds like we'll have a few more folks for you to meet."

"Ricky's boys?" Liam stood taller as he cast an inscrutable glance at the doorway. "Sons or patch brothers?"

"Legends members. Jerry, Ricky and Marilyn's son … my husband, passed away nearly three years ago. He was the only son still in town." Pudgy fingers cradled her jaw, and Ellen looked down at LouCiel. As always, her daughter seemed in tune with her mother's emotions and was looking to comfort her. *Time to end this encounter.* "See you at the table."

With LouCiel's sweet babbling in her ear and tired requests for just one more story, the meal should have been nearly over before Ellen finally made it to the kitchen. Pausing in the doorway, she noted the only empty chair was between Liam and Nick, Dolph's son. Uncomfortable territory, given how Nick couldn't seem to understand the word "no," but Ellen was too hungry to beg off. Plus, she hadn't been lying when she told Liam that Marilyn's cooking wasn't to be missed.

Before she could take more than a step into the room, Liam was on his feet with an empty plate in hand. As the conversation continued to flow, bikers focused on replacement motorcycle parts arguing favorite brands for a variety of things—with a grin, Liam pointed her towards the chair he'd just vacated as he began ladling food on the plate. Puzzled, Ellen took a seat just as he swapped the full plate for the empty one in front of her. Liam settled into the chair next to her, deftly placing himself between her and Nick. Marilyn was opposite Ellen at the table, and when Ellen glanced in her direction, she was entirely failing to hide her grin. Dolph sat at Ricky's right hand, and he looked just as amused, even more so when Nick audibly grumped, "I was gonna make Ellen a plate." Which was a blatant lie because not only hadn't he ever taken that kind of care of her, his normal was more towards asking her to fill his own.

"Thank you, Liam." Ellen ducked her chin to her throat as she took in the offering before her. "That was really kind of you."

"I figured you'd be hungry." The low timbre of her voice rattled her bones, and Ellen clenched down against the sense of emptiness in her chest. "Least I can do for the kindness shown me."

"Oh, I told you earlier, Ricky wouldn't let another soul cold camp in this weather if he can help it. It's no hardship for any of us."

Liam's brow furrowed. "Also, Marilyn might have let slip that I'll be taking your bed tonight. I can roll my bag out on the couch instead, give you back your comfort."

Ellen didn't dare glance at her mother-in-law, not sure what expression she'd see this time. Both Marilyn and Ricky had spent the past year chasing after her to start dating. Not that they wanted her out of their house, because they'd each separately mentioned whoever she selected as her partner would have to be okay living under their roof. Ellen would never cut LouCiel off from her grandparents and loved the fact her daughter got to enjoy both of them every day. *Unlike my own parents.* "I sleep in the second bed in LouCiel's room most of the time anyway. The true guest room doesn't have its own bath, so it made the most sense. It's no bother."

He leaned in closer, and Ellen greedily captured a secretive lungful of his scent. Liam's eyes widened, and she realized maybe her tiny sniff hadn't been quite so covert as she'd thought.

He cleared his throat gruffly. "I appreciate it, Ellen."

The catch in her breathing was entirely automatic at hearing her name on his lips. *Good god, what is wrong with me tonight?* With a tight smile, she nodded and turned her attention to the plate of food he'd prepared for her. *Something a lover or partner would do.* Ellen swallowed hard around the first bite, nearly choking at her thoughts.

"Have you lived here long?" Liam's quiet question startled her, and Ellen looked up to find his gaze trained steadily on her face. "In Grass Creek? Your accent is a little different from Ricky and Marilyn."

"I grew up in Missouri, but I've been up here for eight years." Five good years with Jerry, gaining her feet as an adult. "I love it here."

"What's it like in the other seasons?" Liam's head tilted to the side, a tiny smile playing along his lips.

"Summertime is sunshine for days with blue sky stretching from horizon to horizon. Long twisty roads with the scent of sweetgrass everywhere. Blooms everywhere in the spring." She grinned at him. "It's gorgeous."

"Sounds like it." The corner of his mouth turned up. "Maybe I'll have to find out for myself."

Ellen glanced at Ricky, half expecting to see a disapproving expression, but his face was filled with softness instead. Marilyn cleared her throat, and Ellen looked her way, catching a slow nod of clear approval.

Turning back to Liam, Ellen pulled in a deep breath, gathering her courage. *Time to leap.* "It's the kind of place that really needs a tour guide to find all the best spots."

"You applying for the position?" Liam's expression turned playful, and Ellen gripped her cutlery tighter to keep her hands from straying.

All the boxes in the pros column.

"Maybe." She lifted one shoulder slightly. "Depends on the benefits."

"Oh my God, tell me you didn't just try to pick up Ricky's daughter-in-law at his own table." Nick's derisive tone scraped along Ellen's skin, causing her to curl in on herself.

Ricky spoke up before she could say anything. "Not like you haven't tried the same damn thing, Trashman. Only difference here is—unlike every time you ran up on her in the past two years—I don't hear her telling Irish no."

"He's not even club, man." Nick, a.k.a. Trashman, shoved back from the table. "It's disrespectful to Jerry."

"Pretty sure it's not." Ricky's tone could have frozen a lake. "Also pretty sure if anyone's in a place to say some shit like that, it'd be me, not a prospect. And I'm not givin' off that vibe. You feel me, brother?"

Ellen kept her gaze on Liam during the exchange, somehow not surprised to find his remained latched onto her face in kind. It wasn't that they were ignoring the words, but that whatever this was happening between them wasn't going to be derailed by one man's opinion. Especially when his opinion didn't matter to either of them.

"Marilyn, thanks for dinner." Nick stood and shoved his chair back under the table. "Excellent as always." His face appeared between Ellen and Liam, and she pulled back abruptly. "This isn't the end, Ellen. You're supposed to be mine." His hissed words were meant for her alone, and Ellen shook her head at him. "Don't ignore it."

He was gone before she could compose a response, leaving a swirling mass of emotions in the room.

Dolph sighed heavily. "Sorry about that. Boy got his manners from his mother's side." Ellen tried to smile at his gallows humor, knowing his wife had left when both boys were small and Dolph had raised them alone. "He's mostly a good boy." Wrinkling his nose, he chuckled briefly. "Gets that part from me."

"No worries, Dolph." Liam looked away from Ellen and towards the older man, and she realized it was the first time he'd taken his gaze off her since she'd sat down. "Not to put too fine a point on it, but he's not a boy. He's a grown man, and I'm pretty sure his actions don't negatively reflect on you."

"Kind of you to say." Dolph acknowledged the words with a deep nod. "Marilyn, mind if I get myself a second helping? I've got more questions for Mr. Irish here. That's one sweet bike, and I want to hear all about it."

***

Irish

He'd expected trouble as soon as Dolph and his son had arrived. The younger man had strolled in as if he owned the place, barely greeted Ricky with a lifted chin before puffing his chest out at Irish. "Name's Trashman," he'd declared. "Because I take the trash out." The implication that Irish would be the next piece of trash so handled wasn't lost on him. Not only wasn't it in Irish's nature to be immediately antagonistic and reactionary, but he'd never offer that insult to a host in their own house.

So he'd nodded with a gentle smile, one designed to soothe ruffled feathers, and offered his hand with a "Irish, good to meet friends of Ricky."

During the meal, the asshat had dropped several unsubtle hints that, in his eyes, Ellen was taken. Given the way she'd responded to Irish during their brief interaction, he knew it was a blatant lie and had quietly planned for her entry. After feeding her and putting himself in Trashman's way, Irish had caught both an approving nod from Ricky and a cheeky grin from Marilyn. Those were green lights if he'd ever seen any and firmed his resolve to press his suit.

Once Trashman had blustered his way out of the room, Irish set about seducing the sweet Ellen.

He offered her bits of meat from his fingers, leaned in and forked himself a bite from the edge of her plate, and ensured their shoulders and arms rubbed together nearly constantly. The conversation flowed around the table, filled with talk about bikes and bikers, and shared info about different clubs and rallies.

Finally, after an hour or so, Dolph had laughed at a text on his phone and announced to the table that Nick was cold and tired of waiting in the truck. *Pouting, more like it.* In the flurry of activity surrounding his leave-taking, he leaned close as he clasped Irish's hand and said, "She's a good one. Be careful with our Ellen," and the tacit blessing from someone Ricky clearly trusted made Irish's breath hitch.

"I'll take care of her, my oath on it."

A final pounding slap against his back, and Dolph was gone. Within minutes, both Ricky and Marilyn had retired, leaving Irish to clean the kitchen with Ellen.

While the silence between them was comfortable beyond what it should have been after only a few hours of acquaintance, Irish was ready to find out what could come next.

"I hate knowing I'm putting you out of your own bed." Leaning close, he tapped her shoulder with his chin, resting there for a moment. "Doesn't feel right, making you sleep elsewhere."

"It's no problem, promise." She tilted her face to press her cheek against his, the movement intimate and sweet. "You wouldn't do well on the couch. It wasn't built for sleeping."

"You know…" He hesitated and gave her a beseeching grin. "When I looked at it, it looks like it's a really big bed."

Her hip bumped his, and he caught a glimpse of her return smile. "Is it? I never noticed."

"It is." He stood straight and held up a finger. "I mean, it looks big enough for two. We should try out the theory." Reaching over to take the kitchen towel from her, he hung it up alongside his and grinned, waiting for her teasing comeback.

Ellen lifted her gaze to meet his, her playful expression slowly fading. "I haven't been with anyone since Jerry died." Her hand drifted up, fingertips grazing across the scar along her jaw. "Haven't wanted to test those waters."

"You loved him." Irish pushed certainty into his voice, projecting confidence with his next words. "Wanted to honor him."

"I've been—" Her voice caught and broke. Swallowing hard, she closed her eyes for a breath and then began again. "I've been alone for what feels like forever."

"It's hard, mourning someone worthy of that love. I lost a patch brother last year. Been weighing on me something fierce. I can only imagine the pain when it's a more soulful connection." Irish opened his arms, sighing deeply with the way it felt *right* when Ellen folded herself against his chest. "You don't have to be alone tonight, darlin'. I'm here, and I'll be with you. We don't have to do anything more than this, but I'd like to hold you tonight, if you can see your way clear for that."

Her head rubbed against his shirt, her chin lifting and falling as she wordlessly nodded.

"That's good, then." He tightened his hold on her, somehow not surprised that she fit him perfectly. *Like she was made for me.* "I could use some holding too." Her arms crept around his waist and squeezed. "Yeah, just like that. My momma always said hugs could heal the heart and soul. I never believed her before, but this one just might."

Ellen's laugh was torn through with a hiccuped sob. "Ugh. So sexy, right? Crying is the best."

"Sometimes it's exactly what's needed, you know?" Leaning back slightly, Irish looked down into Ellen's uplifted face. "And I can testify that even wet with tears, your face is gorgeous." His gaze dropped to her lips, and when he met her eyes again, there was a dark heat present. "I'd love to kiss you, Ellen. Think we can go that far?"

Her response was to lift to her toes and press her mouth against his, the caress of her lips trembling and tasting of salt.

Irish started out slowly, testing the texture and softness of her kisses. His tongue slid against her bottom lip, and he groaned when she opened to him, the tip of her tongue meeting his in a glancing glide. Carefully deepening the kiss, Irish slid a hand up, spread fingers cradling the back of her skull. He angled her head and delved further, mapping the movements that pulled sounds from her throat, repeating them until he refined his knowledge of what turned her on.

Ellen's hand wandered up and down the planes of his back, caressing and pressing by turns. When her fingers clutched at the fabric of his shirt, Irish broke the kiss, resting his forehead against hers as they shared quickened breaths. Wide-eyed, Ellen's pupils were blown so the blackness nearly covered the orbs.

"We've privacy just down the hallway. Let's walk that way." Without releasing his hold, Irish steered her backwards, navigating the distance to the bedroom door within moments. "The power is in your hands." He reminded her of what he'd told her before. "If all we do is sleep wrapped up in each other, I'll count it a blessing. Already holding you is easy as breathing and feels just as natural."

"We could start there." Ellen's palms rested on Irish's hips, fingers curving around to grip tightly. "And see where things go from there." The smile she directed his way was soft and warm. "I feel safe with you, Liam."

"High praise." Dipping his mouth to hers again, he found her bolder this time, and it didn't matter whether it was due to familiarity or because they had a locked door between them and the household. *I'll take it.* Knowing she trusted him lit a fire in Irish's belly, a warmth stoked to flames by the connection of mouth and hands. He pulled away with a groan. "Your mouth is fuckin' perfect, darlin'."

Ellen's lips curved into a smile against his. "I like your mouth too." She punctuated the statement with a nip to his bottom lip. "Makes me think wicked things."

"Do tell?" Irish dropped one palm to the curve of her ass, fingers curling possessively around the flesh. "What kind of wicked things, woman?"

"Naked wicked," she responded, body arching into his touch. "The kind of things that make having a big bed a blessing."

Pulling her tight against him, Irish ground his hard cock against her belly, letting her feel his arousal. "I like naked wicked things." Trailing kisses along her cheek, he whispered into her ear, "Tell me more." Alternating kisses and nips, Irish traced the taut tendons in her neck, nuzzling the collar of her shirt to the side in order to mouth along her delicate collarbone. "What wicked things do you want to do, darlin'?"

Breathing quickly, Ellen arched her neck, offering him easy access. "All kinds. So many things. But—*oh*," she gasped when he latched his teeth into the side of her throat. Her voice was hoarser when she continued, "But you're overdressed for all of them."

"Am I?" He found the hem of her shirt and started easing it up, ready to retreat if she offered any hesitancy. "That means you're overdressed too."

"I am," she agreed and lifted her arms as he pulled the shirt over her head.

Gentle light spread into the space from the adjoining bathroom, the door slightly ajar after his quick washup before the meal. It was enough to illuminate everything Irish so desperately wanted to see—the luminous glow of Ellen's skin, her lips kiss-swollen and glistening, eyes still dark with lust. She was so pretty his hands trembled as he traced paths around the edges of her bra, the skin velvet soft.

Pulling her close again, he unfastened and discarded her bra, followed quickly by his vest and shirt. Then they were skin to skin, her soft curves molded against him, the slide and friction exquisite.

"God, Ellen." Irish mouthed the hinge of her jaw, dragging his lips back to her mouth for another deep kiss. "Is this okay?" Given her past and long season of abstinence, he felt compelled to make this a safe space for her. "If you don't want this, at any time, just say so, and we'll stop. Anytime, you hear me? Doesn't matter what we're doing at the time. You say stop and we do."

"I hear you, Liam." Her words were punctuated with soft kisses along his throat. "I'm pretty into this, though. You're... different. You feel different to me." The edge of her teeth scraped along his Adam's apple. "Right." Another teasing graze of teeth. "You feel *right* to me."

Now she was the one steering him towards the bed, pushing at his remaining clothing as if time would get away from them before she had a chance to do whatever was foremost in her mind. It was no hardship to acquiesce, and Irish stripped efficiently, deliberately finding and folding his vest and stacking it on the nearby dresser before toeing off his boots and socks, then dropping his things wherever they landed. He plucked a condom from his wallet, and then both belt and chain wallet rattled as they hit the floor, the abrupt sound pulling a giggle from Ellen. Irish stood with his arms out to the side in silent question, and she giggled again.

"I know it's impolite to discuss previous partners, but that sound, the rattle on the floor, always meant Jerry and I were about to go to pound town. Makes me clench in places I haven't felt in a long time. Pavlovian response, I guess." A tiny, embarrassed shrug lifted one shoulder. "I didn't know I'd missed it like that."

He tossed the condom to the bed as he smiled widely and swooped towards her, wrapping Ellen into his arms, holding her like a treasure. "I have no anxiety surrounding you discussing him, as long as it makes you happy." He popped the button on her jeans and lowered the zipper inch by inch. "But only as long as you're naked with me. That's important protocol."

"Wouldn't want to ignore protocol." Chin lifting, she graced him with a smile. "I don't think I could ever ignore you." Leaning back slightly, she looked him up and down. "Also, there's no ignoring the fact that you're gloriously naked, and I think your little friend likes me."

"Oh, trust me. The entirety of my body wants to say hello, not just my dick." He hissed out a breath when her fingers closed around his cock, giving it a long, slow stroke up and down. "You keep that kind of thing up and this'll be over in about point two seconds." A slow breath in was broken when her fingertips plucked at his sack, tugging slightly as he shuddered with want. "Seriously, Ellen, it's been a while for me too."

"Means you have more than one in you then, right?"

When he nodded at her question, certainty spread over her features, and he leaned his forehead against hers. Then, as he attempted to focus on removing her clothing, Ellen set about teasing and torturing him. Cock hard as steel in her sure grip, his balls drew up tighter with each delicate pluck and tug, bringing him closer to the heat building at the base of his spine.

When she had to stop and step out of her clothing, he breathed deeply and circled his fingers at the base of his cock painfully hard, staving off the orgasm threatening to blow his world apart.

Mock frowning, she tut-tutted at his handiwork and sidled closer, pressing her silk-soft skin against every inch of his front. "I was having fun, Liam."

"And you can still have fun." He scooped her up bridal-style, took two steps towards the bed, and tossed her to the mattress. Her giggle as she bounced made his heart skip a beat. *What is it about this woman?* "We'll just be horizontal as we do fun, wicked, naked things together."

Prowling up the mattress towards her, he stretched out over her, pressing a gentle knee between her thighs as he propped himself up on one elbow.

"I like the idea of naked fun," she reminded him. Her fingertips ghosted across his flanks and sides, a gentle up and down drawing goose bumps to the surface of his skin. "I want to please you, Liam."

"I have no doubt we'll both be well pleased by morning." Up this close, he glimpsed faint freckles dusting the skin of her nose and cheeks and dropped kisses along the same path. "You're so pretty, Ellen. A good mom, too."

"That's an attractive trait?" She sounded dubious, so he nodded.

"Yeah, it is. Knowing a woman has that kinda love inside her is hot as hell."

She laughed and angled her head, offering up her lips, and he accepted, kissing her gently. Within moments, the kiss turned fantastically dirty, with sliding tongues and gasps for air. He bit at her lips until they were glistening, then dove back in for another deep kiss, fingers tangled in her hair as he cradled the back of her skull, holding her to him.

Ellen moved underneath him, her body lifting like a wave as he pressed his thigh between her legs, giving her a firm surface to grind her pussy against.

"Oh." She pulled back on a gasp, and with eyes fluttering closed, tilted her hips up and down, slicking his skin with her wetness.

He slipped a hand between them, gliding along her gently rounded belly to the tightly curled thatch of dark hair at the juncture of her thighs. Already knowing she was wet, he reveled in the explosive heat of her. Laying his mouth over hers again, they kissed more slowly, lips and tongues exploring as he stroked and teased her.

Time stretched out, spinning into nothingness because there wasn't anything more important than these primary points of connection between them. Rubbing a fingertip between her lower lips, he circled the nub of flesh rich with nerve endings, hips moving in time with hers as she arched into his touch, and he sought friction against the curve of her hip.

His middle finger slipped inside, and he curled it, thrusting gently against her tight heat. Knowing how much better that constrictive fire was going to feel around his cock took Irish's breath, and he broke the kiss for a moment to stare down into Ellen's face. The expression of pleasure was marred for an instant by a frown, then she explained the look with one demanding word.

"More."

A second finger joined the first and her gasp was music, trailing from her lips to light up his mind with pleasure. *Giving her what she wants. What she needs.*

"Please, Liam, more."

The effect of his name on her lips was like a bomb going off in his belly, warmth and excitement flowing through him. Irish bent his neck and clamped lips around a nipple, drawing hard against her flesh as her hips rose to meet his every movement.

"So good, Liam." Breathy and soft, she encouraged him with words and actions, her hands finding the back of his head to hold him in place, urging him to ravish her breast as he'd already treated her mouth. He trapped the nipple between his teeth, lashing it with his tongue to draw a moan from her. Sucking again, he pulled more of her into his mouth before moving his lips to the side of her breast and latching on again, laying sucking kisses to leave a line of marks on her skin.

He moved down her body, pressing kisses on every section of skin, nibbling on her hip bones, dancing his tongue in the grooves where hips met torso, listening to the sounds he pulled from her throat with each action. Her pussy grew impossibly wetter, slickness paving the way for his thrusting digits, tip of his thumb flicking against her clit with every sequence of movements.

His other hand remained on her breast, pinching and kneading, caressing, and coveting each inch of flesh.

When his mouth zeroed in on her center, tongue lapping at the delicious feast of pleasure she'd provided, her gasp echoed through the room.

"Oh, Liam." Staring up the line of her body to her face, he watched as desire warred with embarrassment on her features. "You don't have to. I haven't washed up."

"Mmmmm." He punctuated his approving sounds with a slurping suck, engulfing as much of her vulva and clit as possible. "Mmmmm." Repeating the deep hum, he pressed deeper, tongue finding the entrance he sought so he could fuck her with fingers and tongue for long minutes, cataloging every movement and sound.

"God. Oh bless—" A ragged breath and her strangled words exposed how much she was enjoying his ministrations. "Liam, I'm going to—"

Ellen's body tensed under his hands and mouth, hips arching away from the mattress as she softly keened. She gave him her orgasm, her body trusting that he'd care for her through the experience, and he did. Working fingers and mouth to pull additional shuddering moans for extended moments as he exploited all the places he'd mapped.

Kneeling between her legs, he made quick work of the condom before leaning over her, palm to the curve of her cheek. "Ellen, darlin', you with me?"

"Mmhmm." The murmur purred lazily across her lips, features soft in repose.

He paused. "Wanna sleep now?" If all he got was what had happened so far, he'd leave Grass Creek a happy man. Knowing he'd brought her to the edge and got her to fly like she had was glorious all on its own.

She blinked, hooded eyes staring up at him as a smile curled the corners of her lips. "Not a chance, big man."

"Well, alrighty then." He chuckled darkly at her seductive expression and sure tone. "Prepare yourself for a ride, darlin'."

With a hand pressing gently against the inside of each knee, he spread her legs wider, gaze devouring every inch of her. Light and darkness warred all along her torso, concealing and exposing each delicious curve. Silver scars mottled and streaked along her belly and thighs, the top slope of her breasts, and he made a note to love on those especially well. He hadn't been joking earlier when he told her the adoration she had for her daughter was a draw, and now seeing her proudly bear the marks of the journey that had brought her to this moment settled in his soul. *She's special. Not just to me, but maybe especially to me.*

Bending double, he buried his mouth against her clit again, smiling against her flesh when Ellen gave first a startled gasp and then a soft moan of arousal. Sucking and licking fiercely for a moment, he then gentled his approach, leaving that part of her body with a chaste kiss. Moving up across her belly, he brought his desires to truth as he kissed every mark he could find.

Adjusting his body to fall between her thighs, Irish planted his elbows on the mattress on either side of her chest, using his hands to bring her breasts together. Turning his head side to side, he placed sucking kisses on each, dragging the edge of his teeth across the nipples until she twisted restlessly beneath him, hips arching up to grind her clit against his belly.

"Liam?" Her voice held a note of querulous inquiry, impatience in every letter. "I'm ready."

Smiling against the nipple clamped between his teeth, he shook his head slightly before going back to his self-assigned tasks.

"I am. I want you. Ohhhh." The way her words ended on a rising moan reflected the success of his work.

"Patience, Ellen." He lifted his mouth long enough to flash her a grin. "I'm moving at my own pace." *Dictated by your body, but that goes without saying.*

"Well, your pace is slower than molasses." The complaint lost its heat as her entire body shuddered when he moved higher between her legs, latex-covered cock nudging at her entrance. "Yes, please."

"As my lady wishes." Pushing up on his arms, Irish curved his back, hips shifting closer. When she reached between them, the heated clasp of her fingers nearly undid him as she brought them together. Another tiny adjustment and the head of his dick rested exactly where they both wanted it. Gentle undulations of his hips worked him inside, fractions of an inch at a time.

Irish was entranced by every expression flitting across her face. Surprise, followed by desire, a flash of fear and sorrow, then another warm moment of desire, mouth falling open on a moan.

Without surprise, Irish realized he could spend the rest of his life gazing down on her and never get tired of the delicious view.

***

Ellen

The way Liam held his body above her, as if afraid his weight would crush and mangle her, made Ellen laugh softly.

His head cocked to the side at the sound, the puzzled question clear on his features.

"Come here," she urged, hands pulling at his shoulder and hip. "Let me feel you. I won't break."

"Ah." He resisted her pull, and his smile in response was gentle, holding an edge of affection she hadn't expected. "Maybe I like the view from here."

Ellen deliberately clenched around his generously sized cock, and Liam's eyes closed. His Adam's apple bobbed twice before he opened his eyes again, staring down at her with a rush of heat, dark gaze focused on her face. She clenched again.

"You win this time, Ellen." Moving each arm in turn, he settled his weight on her, hips never losing their rhythm and movement. "But one day I'll make love to you stretched out like that, so I can see every inch of your pleasure."

The "one day" caught her breath and hope bloomed inside her.

"I think we both win, at least I hope so."

He made an agreeable sound as he tucked his head in next to hers, mouth moving along the side of her neck.

It was impossible to explain how this felt so right, so Ellen didn't try to overthink or dissect it. For the first time in a long time, she gave herself permission to just feel.

Safe.

His big arms curved around her, holding her close. With the way he wrapped her up by his muscled body, he became a barrier against the world, protecting her and this space against anything.

Desired.

The hardness thrusting inside her was unmistakable proof that Liam wanted her, but the way he'd loved on her carried it to a different plane. This wasn't sex for the sake of getting off. This was more. It had started the first time their gazes met and been fed with every encounter through the few hours they'd had together so far, building to a blaze that threatened to burn her to the ground with the heat of his lovemaking.

Seen.

Not something she'd expected to need, but the way he'd paid attention to everything was a balm to her soul. From offering her extra bites of food he'd noted she liked to the way he'd paid homage to the stretchmarks from carrying LouCiel, it was as if he'd mapped her with mind, fingers, and tongue. That kind of attention was heady, rich with possibility she hadn't expected to find in her life again. The potential for a deep and true love.

Loved.

Warm breaths brushed the curve of her ear as lips pressed soft kisses on her cheek, unshaven scruff a delicious counterpoint. He neither avoided nor sought out the scar on her face, just dropped kisses along her jaw. As if that moment in time didn't define her. As if she continued to live and grow and be. And Ellen *believed*. It was possible to find love after loss. She knew this truth in her gut, even if a day ago she'd never have thought it possible.

Arms and legs wrapped tightly around him, Ellen held Liam closely. Body already primed from his earlier ministrations, another orgasm was already building low in her belly, drawing more sounds from her as her body clenched around him. They fit together so well, him dwarfing her just enough that she could anchor her heels around the backs of his thighs, lifting her hips to add extra power to each of his thrusts.

"Ellen." Liam's soft murmur against the flesh of her throat drew goose bumps to every inch of her skin. "Ellen, Ellen, Ellen. So good."

"Yes." She could only gasp out her agreement, breath stolen by the force of the feelings sweeping through her.

Faster now, his cock shuttled in and out as every muscle she owned tightened. Another deep push, another undulation of his hips, and she was there, rising from the top of the cliff and hovering for a moment before plummeting, safe in the knowledge that Liam would catch her. His chest heaved against hers, each of his breaths coming on a groan as his movements lost their rhythm. Body curving around her, encompassing her, Liam stiffened, and his cock kicked inside her. By the third or fourth hard, hot pulse into the condom, he clasped her tighter, mouth trailing across the scar on her jaw to find her mouth. They kissed desperately, tongues sliding, sharing breaths as he finished coming, still buried deep in her body.

Gradually the kiss slowed, nips becoming more of a tease than the branding bites of earlier, lips slipping slowly against each other in long glides. Finally, Liam broke the connection, resting his forehead against hers, and she fluttered her eyes open to find him staring solemnly at her.

Afraid to speak, Ellen didn't dare chance breaking whatever spell had controlled them both.

Liam had no such qualms.

"Ellen." Soft and gruff, his voice stroked across the butterflies in her belly, stirring them to more agitation. "Got a connection with you. Never felt anything like it. Knew from the moment I saw you that you were special, but I didn't have any idea of exactly how right I was. Feels like I've been with you forever, but with the excitement of our first time."

"I feel it too," she admitted, keeping her gaze fixed on his. "It's good."

"And fast." His smile curved against her lips as they kissed again, a brief caress. "But fast doesn't scare me, not with this."

"I've got considerations—"

"Lucy and Jerry's folks." His response was quick, cutting her off as he laid out his understanding for her. "Of course they're in this too, in different ways. We try this out, pull each other on for size, they're part of it all. You're doing everything right, keeping Lucy first and caring for family. Not gonna get any argument outta me on that front."

"When I met Jerry, it was quick, but we both knew. I picked up and left home, came here, and Marilyn and Ricky adopted me immediately. My own folks were mad. Still are." And that stung more than she'd expected. By the quick frown on Liam's brow, she knew those feelings had been clear in her tone. "I don't blame them, not for their first disappointment. They'd wanted a lot for me, had planned things for my future. My rebellion wasn't expected, and they didn't react well, and then I didn't give them a chance to get used to the idea before I was gone."

"They ever seen Lucy?" With a single question, Liam dove straight to the crux of her continued anger at her parents.

She shook her head in answer, and his expression darkened, growing stormy. He buried his face in her neck, arms tight around her again as he wordlessly comforted her.

"Their loss, right?" Tight and small, her whisper barely broke the silence.

"Entirely their loss. I'm glad you have Jerry's folks to love on you and Lucy, show her how family is supposed to be and act." He sighed heavily. "I don't have anything like what Ricky's got with his club. Nothing to leave behind, really."

Until his words, she hadn't acknowledged the fear nipping at her thoughts. All the "what ifs" of how this might work out.

"You were headed to Bozeman?"

"Yeah." The single word had weight and Ellen braced herself. "Give me a minute and I'll tell you why."

Liam propped himself on an elbow and reached between them, anchoring the condom to his dick as he pulled his now soft cock out. Taking a moment to deal with the condom, he came back from the bathroom with a wet cloth, gently tending to her before tossing it back to the tiled floor.

Knee-walking his way up the bed, he lifted her shoulders to slide an arm underneath so he could draw her to face him as he stretched out and pulled the covers up. They weren't quite nose-to-nose, but she could feel the warm gusts of his breathing against her skin.

"Had a brother pass. Last year. We were close, ride or die, brother from another kind of relationship. I said left and he was already turning. He'd say go and I'd be right behind. We were real close. Losin' him has been hard. Took something outta me I didn't know I had, and try as I might, back home I couldn't quite wrap my head around him not being around anymore." With closed eyes, Liam's head traveled side to side as he paused for a moment. "Lyon was a good man. Really good. Made me a better brother. Hell, Ly made me a better man."

Liam's words stopped for long enough Ellen wasn't certain he'd continue. She asked, "And Bozeman?"

"His folks are from there. Some family plot that came with expectations. So his mom took his ashes home and laid him to rest there. I was headed up to pay my respects. Tell the bastard how pissed I am he's gone." A broken laugh tore from his lips, slicing Ellen's heart. "Son of a bitch wasn't supposed to die."

"Grief is hard." Ellen's experience made her words certain. "Doesn't matter the how, because just the fact of the loss is enough to change a person. Losing someone you love, no matter how that relationship binds you together, is an emotional amputation, and the phantom pains come unexpectedly. They'll rule your life for days at a time, then slide to the background for a bit before coming on strong, like a storm. With grief, there's no one-size-fits-all solution either." She arched closer, cupping one hand around his throat, the rapid thudding of his heartbeat pounding against her palm. "Different people grieve the same person differently, dictated by whatever connection they had. The fact you're still grieving your brother a year down the road just tells me that you were bound. Not by blood but by experience and trust. That's strong, Liam. Nothing to be embarrassed about there. Strong love is a blessing, however it comes about."

"No lies in those words. Like I was saying about Ricky and Marilyn, it's good to have people where you belong. I'd never ask you to give that up."

Ellen's nerves had her heart thudding hard, and she blinked back threatening tears. The only way she'd know if Liam was serious would be to ask, straight out.

Before she could, he laid each of her fears to rest.

"You want to explore this, I'd leave the east coast, come here, and find a place, a job. This between us feels right, and if you're open, then I'd be ready now."

"After a few hours and a single round of sex? You'd uproot your entire life?"

"I'd argue what we just shared wasn't just a 'round of sex,' but yes, there's a promise of so much good here, I'd be an idiot not to want to see where it leads. The distance would be a barrier, and I'd be damned before I let you leave Lucy's grandparents behind. Good thing is I got enough skills to find a job easy. After we lost Lyon, the club's become a burden. It'll almost be a relief to lay my colors down. Wouldn't even ask for nomad, just thank them for their time. I'm all paid up on my dues, so there's nothing barring me leaving."

His next kiss was softer, tender, as if he knew she needed gentle handling through the panic threatening to swamp her.

"And you? After only a few hours and a session of sweet, sweet love, are you ready to give this a try? You've got more skin in the game because Lucy is such an important person. I can promise to only be to her whatever you allow. You want me to be Mommy's special friend, I'll make it happen. Uncle Irish? That'd be good, too. Something as significant as that needs to be deliberate and unrushed. Handled with care."

Nodding slowly, Ellen reached out, needing the feel of his skin under her palm. She rested her hand over the smooth curve of his pec, muscles rising and falling with each of his steady breaths. Just feeling how calm he was soothed her, gave her a sense of determination to not lose this fledgling connection that had started growing between them.

"I can't imagine losing this—you—now. It's fast but doesn't feel impetuous. Doesn't feel like a knee-jerk reaction to an attraction. I mean, there's attraction plenty, but that's not all that's here. There's a promise of so much more between us." Ellen grinned, wrinkling her nose at the memories of the unsubtle signals at dinner. "Pretty sure we've got the blessings of those I count as family, so that's a barrier we don't have to worry about."

"Yeah." His deep chuckle rumbled underneath her touch, and she snuggled closer, tilting her head to keep his face in view. "Pretty sure everyone at that table except Trashman had an idea where this might be headed."

"Nick's a pain in the ass for everyone, not just you." Ellen didn't try to stop the slight eye roll accompanying her words. "Jerry said he'd tried to mentor him, but the kid was just so determined to be the big man on campus, he couldn't see how little it really made him."

"Wise words." Liam's mouth brushed her forehead, the soft kiss feeling like a benediction. "This is nice, Ellen. Just holding you feels good." His arms flexed, tightening for a moment before relaxing. "You feel good."

"I do?" She let an edge of playfulness creep into her tone, encouraged when the corner of his mouth tipped up.

"Mmhmm." He pulled her closer again, holding the grip for longer. "Real good, Ellen."

Bending her neck, she placed a soft kiss at the base of his throat. "I bet I could make it even better." Another kiss.

"Oh yeah?" He arched, giving her more access she immediately exploited.

"Oh, yeah." One hand on his shoulder levered him to his back, and she rolled so he partially supported her weight. "I have ideas."

"Woman, I already know you have good ideas, so you just go on ahead with whatever you want to do." One of his hands flattened between her shoulder blades, and the other curved around a cheek of her ass with a squeeze. "Just know that I plan on playing too."

"I'd expect no less." Sliding down the bed, she let the sheet cover her head as she trailed kisses down his chest and belly. "You do you, boo."

***

Irish

Ellen's soft lips pressed against the edge of his hip, angling across his body, and Irish's muscles tightened, cock twitching hopefully. *Best manage expectations.*

"Darlin', I see your play here, and I'm gonna love all of it, but don't be disappointed if you don't get the reaction you want. I'm not a teenager anymore, not by a long shot. I know I promised I had more than one in me tonight, but it takes me a while in between, you know?"

Her laughter was interrupted by more kisses to his skin and held no edge of taunting to it. Irish smiled down at the sheet-covered lump hovering over his groin as he rested a hand on the back of her head.

"I'm going to indulge myself then, if you don't mind."

"Mind? What the hell kind of man would mind a gorgeous woman wanting to touch him? Not caring if he couldn't get hard? That's not something I'm gonna turn down." He lifted the sheet and peered down at her, not surprised to find her gaze lifted to him. Intense and beautiful, she gave him a quirked grin. "Fuckin' gorgeous, Ellen. You take my breath away."

She rolled her eyes and bent her head. The first hot lick along the shaft made his legs jerk. She treated his cock like a favorite dessert, tonguing the length before placing open-mouthed kisses and licks all over the head. He groaned when she caressed his balls while teasing the slit at the tip, the sensitive sensations riding the line between not enough and too much.

"Feels good, Ellen. Loving your ideas."

She hummed in appreciation, mouth snuggled in at the base of his cock. With another slow glide of her tongue up his semihard dick, Ellen closed her lips around the head and sucked. Softly at first, tongue fluttering along the underside until his cock twitched again, harder, blood rushing from his head to his groin and pulling the semi closer to a full hardness.

Another tug at his balls lent the bite of pain to the pleasure, and he groaned, watching as she took him in her mouth, the entirety of his cock encircled by the heat and movement, the suction from her tight lips around the base of his shaft, and glide of her tongue.

It didn't take long for the length of his dick to outgrow her mouth, and Irish had to choke back a shout when he felt the back of her throat constrict around the head. Eyes watering as she cut off her own air, he was surprised at her determination to bring him pleasure.

"Ellen."

Eyes closed in concentration, she didn't look up at him. He flipped the sheet out of the way, needing to see everything.

Fingers gliding through her hair, he tangled his grip in the strands and tugged gently.

"Ellen."

She came off his dick with a lewd pop, tongue darting out to lap at the tip. With tear-clumped lashes, she lifted her gaze. The spots of color in her cheeks and impish grin told him she'd been enjoying herself nearly as much as he'd been.

"Yeah?"

The rasp of her voice, altered from the smooth tenor earlier, shot a rough spike of arousal through him and his dick jumped in her hand. She'd done that, taking him deep, wrecked her own throat to give him pleasure.

"Goddamn, woman, you are sexy as fuck." He tightened his hold when she rolled her eyes dismissively. "Not fuckin' around here, Ellen. You're dead sexy all the time, but right now, kneeling between my legs and worshipin' my cock? Fuckin' hell. I'm a seriously lucky man."

"I'll take your word for it." The tip of her tongue circled the mushroom ridge. "And." Ellen shifted position, tilting her head into the hold he had on her hair. "As much as I've been enjoying myself here, I think I was promised a round two." Crawling up the bed, careful of where she placed elbows and knees, she paused when she hovered over him. Bending her head so her mouth was a fraction of an inch away, she whispered, "Do you mind kissing, after?"

He answered with actions, guiding her head the rest of the way so they connected firmly. Then he separated her lips with a swipe of his tongue, chasing the taste of himself into her mouth. Rough and raw, this kiss was less of an exploration and more statement of fact. He wanted her, full stop.

Heat enveloped his dick where it lay on his belly, and he bit at her lips, driven wild by her need, expressed with her body. Arching his hips up, he met every swipe of her pussy along his cock with firm pressure, letting her ride him this way. Wetness spread along the length of him, evidence of her rising passion, and he slipped a hand between them to capture some on his fingers.

One hand spreading her ass, he dipped the slippery fingertips into the crease, finding and circling the sensitive, puckered opening there. Ellen gasped in his ear and keened out his name.

"Liam."

When the tip of a finger breached the ring of muscles, she moved with intent, battering herself backwards and forwards, lips of her pussy clasping along the root and shaft of his cock on every slide while she humped against his finger.

"Oh, oh. Liam. Please."

A flurry of words accompanied a sheen of sweat on her skin, and Irish turned his head to capture her mouth in a gasping, sucking kiss that managed to be both sloppy and intense.

She tensed, muscles tightening as she shuddered, her head dropping to his shoulder with a cry. Irish adjusted his grip on her, wrapping his arms around her back, holding her close as she rode out her orgasm.

Slowly relaxing, she stretched out a leg and rolled slightly to the side, keeping close contact between their bodies as her head found a pillow on his chest.

"Just." Breathing hard, she panted out the words. "Give me a minute. That was epic."

Irish grinned widely and bent his neck, kissing the top of her head. "Take your time, darlin'. You're worth any wait, promise. Plus—" He stroked a hand down her spine. "—it was a good show. Enjoyed watching you take yourself there. Something I hope to see again and again."

"It was so good." With a big sigh, she lifted her head. "Hard to believe this time yesterday I didn't even know you."

"I know. Kismet, maybe." Irish shrugged as he threaded a hand through her tousled hair. "Can't imagine things being different."

"Thank God for a blown tire?" Ellen smiled and leaned down to kiss his chest, then wiggled up so she could rest her face against his throat, arm around his waist. "I've never been a believer in fate before."

"First time for everything." Irish rolled them, placing Ellen on her back in the middle of the bed. "I've been trusting in karma for a while, putting good things out into the world, knowing that somehow, sometime, they'd come back to me."

"So I'm your karma?" Palm fitted to his face, she studied him. "I kinda like that idea."

"Me too." Dipping to kiss her, Irish lost himself in the sensation until they were both breathless. "Be right back." Slipping from the bed, he grabbed his bag and retrieved another condom.

"We can talk about those at some point." Ellen took it from him and held it with one hand, the other reaching out to wrap around his dick. She stroked his flagging erection back to full strength, then opened the wrapper and rolled the latex down his cock, giving the root a final hard squeeze. "But I appreciate you taking care with me."

"I think takin' care of you is gonna be second nature." Irish positioned himself between her knees, widening his stance to spread her open. "Never gonna get tired of this view."

Ellen crooked her fingers at him with a grin. "Well, enjoy it from a little closer. Wanna feel you, Liam. Want you inside me."

"Won't say no to that invitation." With his forearms propped on either side of her head, he stole a kiss as she arched her hips up against him. In seconds, he was notched at her entrance, slowly thrusting inside her hot, tight channel. "So good for me."

"Yeah?" Her eyes fluttered open, having closed at his first push. "It's good for me too. Hard and huge, stretching me in all the right ways."

His balls drew up and his cock pulsed until Irish had to stop moving. "I didn't know sexy talk did it for me." His chuckle was soft, breathy, broken as he pressed kisses to her lips, her jaw, across her cheeks. "But maybe it's the whole package that's stealin' my control."

"If you don't move—" Punctuating her words with a lift of her hips, Ellen huffed out a laugh. "I'm gonna steal all your control." She clenched around him, and Irish's hips stuttered back and forth of their own volition.

"You know that's not really a threat, right?" Murmuring against the side of her head, Irish let himself move again, thrusting in deep and hard, followed by a slow out stroke with a pause at the end before snapping his hips forward again. "I'd gladly give you the reins at some point."

"Just not yet." Ellen's voice was like rough silk as she spoke around teeth clenched in his shoulder. "God, Liam. So good. You love me so good."

I do.

The thought spurred him onwards, sure knowledge driving him to bring her to the edge and over one more time.

"Tell me when you're close, darlin'." Sweat slicked the slide of their bodies, and Irish curled a hand underneath her, squeezing her ass hard, spreading his fingers across both cheeks, then dipping between.

One of her hands slipped across his belly, and he lifted slightly, giving her easier access to her clit. The brush of her fingers against his root was toe-curling good and added sensation to an already brilliant round of loving.

"I'm there, Liam."

"Go, baby. Go."

Turning his head, he sought and found her mouth, kissing her through the moans wrenched from her by the orgasm that stiffened her muscles and drew her pussy tight around his dick. Slowing his movements, he rode her through the waves of pleasure until she slumped underneath him, legs loosely draped over his thighs. Once he was certain she'd wrung everything from her orgasm, he picked up the pace again.

Hand behind one of her knees, he lifted the leg to his hip, the different angle pushing him farther inside her. Powerful strokes carried him in and out, and it took only moments until his balls lifted tight to his body, the electric bolts of ecstasy spreading out from his spine to every inch of his skin.

Forehead to her shoulder, he let the sensation sweep him away, the tight hold of her arms and hands anchoring him in the moment. Heat surrounded the head of his cock as he flooded the condom, blindly resentful of that barrier as he'd never been before.

Someday. That was the only word he let himself think before sinking down to blanket her body with his own.

"Ellen."

Her hands brushed up and down his back, fingers stroking his spine and ribs, rising to thread through his hair.

"I've got you." Her words were soft, but the meaning profound. "I've got you, Liam."

This time it was Ellen who slipped from the bed and took care of the condom, bringing back a warm, wet cloth to clean his face and throat, washing his chest and belly before cleaning his cock with care.

A moment later, he had an armful of warm, wiggling woman as she snuggled close, one leg thrown over his thighs as she returned her head to the pillow of his chest.

"Night, Liam."

He smiled into the darkness, arm curled around her shoulders, fingers threaded through hers on his belly.

"Night, Karma."

Testing the Edges

Ellen

Waking slowly, Ellen stretched luxuriously, the stretch of every muscle telling her that last night hadn't been a dream. But she was alone. Stretching out a hand, she found Liam's side of the bed still slightly warm, which meant he hadn't been gone long.

Rolling to the side of the bed, she stretched again, then quickly dressed and tidied the room, a token to her normal routine. A glance at her phone told her she was behind in her schedule, and LouCiel should have already been pounding at the door. *Maybe she slept in too?*

She cracked the door and peeked out to see the one just down the hall was also open. On the off chance LouCiel was quietly playing in her room, Ellen took the two steps to reach the entrance and stealthily leaned her head around the doorframe to see inside.

Liam was crouched behind where LouCiel sat on her stool. She was prattling on about something, only a word here and there loud enough for Ellen to catch. Liam was sweeping a brush through one half of LouCiel's hair, the other already caught up in a pigtail.

"Tell me if I hurt you, Lucy." Liam's murmur made LouCiel shake her head, thwarting his efforts. Instead of scolding her like Ellen likely would have done, he laughed softly and started the process again. It took a couple more tries, but eventually, he finished and LouCiel sprang off the stool like a pogo stick, twirling and throwing her arms around his neck, nearly unbalancing him in the process.

"T'ank yous," her little girl crowed, the uneven pigtails bouncing with every movement. "T'ank yous berry much."

"It's beautiful. And you're very welcome. Now, let's go get you some breakfast, princess." Liam groaned dramatically as he rose to his feet, LouCiel still in his arms. "And I need some coffee."

Ellen leaned into the room with a wave. "Morning, you two."

"Mommy!" LouCiel didn't release her hold on Liam's neck. "He fixed my hairs. Said he couldn't, but then he did it all by himself." LouCiel's head shook violently, and she nearly slammed against Liam's jaw before he could react. "Me pretty."

"Yes you are." Ellen stepped closer. "You could have woken me." With emotions from the night before still flooding through her and the scene she'd just witnessed, Ellen couldn't imagine hiding this, any of it, from the people she loved. Rolling to her toes, she placed a kiss on the underside of Liam's jaw. "But I appreciate the extra sleep."

An arm slipped around her waist, pulling her flush against his chest. LouCiel shifted to one hip as he drew them into a three-way hug.

"My pleasure, darlin'."

She smiled against his shirt, sharing a look across his strong chest with LouCiel whose mouth fell open dramatically, then morphed into the biggest smile the child could manage.

"I likes dis." Her little girl snuggled closer, curling against Liam so her head rested on his shoulder. "Dis is nice."

"Yeah, it is," Liam agreed with a laugh rumbling through his chest, the happy vibrations making Ellen smile wider. "But I still need coffee."

"Priorities, I know." Ellen pulled back and held her hands up. "Come here, monster. We'll give Liam a break and let him get his caffeine fix."

"Nope." LouCiel's arms visibly tightened around Liam's neck. "Me fines ri here."

"Breakfast, right, princess?" Liam winked at Ellen as she stepped away, shaking her head. "Gotta feed my girls."

Ellen's breath caught in her chest as that statement warmed her inside and out. Her voice wavered as she forced out, "Sounds like a plan." *His girls.*

At Liam's questioning glance, she shook her head and shot him a beaming smile that seemed to reassure him. His warm hand settled at the small of her back, steering her towards the hallway and kitchen. The possessive action acted to reassure her too, reminding Ellen she wasn't alone in this brand-new exploration of what could be between them.

That led to an almost perfect Christmas Eve. Snow started midmorning, and Ricky built a fire in the living room, the massive fireplace mantle filled with pictures of the family. Liam was attentive, staying close, interacting with LouCiel in ways that made Ellen's eyes sting with tears. She caught Ricky and Marilyn exchanging dopey smiling glances several times. It wasn't until Ricky went to plug in the Christmas tree that Marilyn caught Ellen in the kitchen, making cider and hot chocolate for them all, that she had a moment alone with her mother-in-law.

"I like him for you." Marilyn was blunt as was her way, and for once, Ellen was glad she didn't beat around the bush. "I like him for Lucy. Hell, I just like him. He's good with Ricky, too, and that's a feat. Boy's a keeper, my girl."

Marilyn's arms encircled her, and Ellen turned to embrace her in return.

"I like him." Ellen let herself voice the thoughts that had been racing through her head all day. "It's so fast, but it feels like forever at the same time."

"You're like me in a lotta ways, daughter-in-love. When you know, you know, and there's no amount of talking or fussing that's gonna change what your heart says." Marilyn's arms tightened possessively. "Did you tell him you're never leaving us?"

Nodding and laughing, Ellen choked out, "I did, and he immediately told me exactly how he can make that happen. It's perfect. *He's* perfect. And so sweet to LouCiel."

"He sees her as her own person, not a childish extension of you. That's not something that can be faked. I get the sense he likes us all, individually. Likes you more, obviously." Marilyn pinched her ass, and Ellen squeaked and pulled away. "You get you a little somethin' somethin' last night?"

Ellen's face heated, and Marilyn laughed at her intoxicated giggle. "Maybe, but that's not something I'm going to share."

"Not one to kiss and tell? I like it. Smart girl." Marilyn's hands gripped hers as the smile faded from her lips. "This is me, standing here in our family home and telling you that this is a good thing, Ellen. This is something Ricky and I both support, as long as it's what you want. I'm sure Ricky's going to give him the 'hurt our girl and you'll never be found' speech soon, but I wanted you to know we're *happy* for you."

"I love that about you both. I'm so lucky to have you in my life...in LouCiel's life. I just love you."

"Sucks that Jerry died. Sucks harder he never got to really experience what being a daddy is about. Sucks for you and sucks for Lucy. I'm not saying Irish will ever take his place, but I think there's a new place here that fits him just right. What doesn't suck is that you might get a second chance at love. *That* doesn't suck." Marilyn shook her hands and leaned in, placing a kiss on Ellen's forehead. "And it doesn't suck that he's fine to look at either."

"Marilyn!" Ellen was surprised into a laugh. "But you aren't wrong on any of those points."

"I'm old, but I still got eyes." Marilyn gave her a sly glance. "Just don't tell my old man."

"I'd never rat you out." Ellen kept her eyes wide, foiling the tears that threatened. "We'd better finish the hot chocolate, or someone's going to check on us."

Returning to the living room was like walking into a fantasy. The tree blinked and flashed, fire clucking quietly to itself on the hearth, and her heart and soul was cuddled on Liam's lap, gaze turned up to his face adoringly. He was in the middle of a story, complete with movements and sound effects, and LouCiel was eating it up. As Ellen came closer, she heard the name Rudolph and realized instead of a motorcycle trip tale, he was giving her a Christmas memory.

Liam looked up, and without missing a beat, held out the arm opposite where he held LouCiel tightly. Ellen snuggled in beside him on the couch, his arm lightly across her shoulders as she fell just a little harder for this man.

***

Irish

Lucy's nose had been plastered to the front window as soon as full dark had fallen, looking for Santa. A few minutes after she'd been ushered off to bed with promises of being woken if anyone laid eyes on the jolly old elf, Ellen and Marilyn had pulled a box of prewrapped presents out of the older couple's bedroom.

Liam found himself with batteries and a screwdriver in hand, putting the final touches on a simple remote-control car. Being included in the traditions, even in a small way, touched him, and it was with gruff thanks he returned the toy and controller to Ricky. The man gave him a wry grin and a knock on his shoulder with a muttered, "You'll get used to it."

Once everything was arranged to Marilyn's satisfaction, she snapped her fingers in Ricky's direction and demanded, "Drinks."

"Ma'am, yes, ma'am." Ricky popped a salute that spoke of military experience and made his way towards the sideboard, where there were bottles and glasses on the top shelf. "Whatever the love of my life desires."

Liam watched the interaction between the couple with amusement when Ellen's arm slipped around his waist, fingers of her other hand twining with his. She lifted his arm around her own shoulders and looked up at him with a smile.

"Fair warning. These two are my best examples of marital bliss, so buckle up, bucko." She squinted her eyes at him in mock threat. "Marky are couple goals."

"Marky?" He questioned reflexively before the fact it was a shipped name registered. "Oh, Marilyn plus Ricky equals Marky. Got it." He pulled her tight against his side, relishing the way she fit there. "So, you want a snarky, half-seriously-in-love, half-want-to-kill-each-other, tolerant, affectionate relationship?"

"Exactly." She sighed softly and tipped her head to rest against his shoulder. Marilyn and Ricky had continued sparring, warring now over the ratio of ice to scotch needed. "Watch, she'll take over in three, two—"

"Good God, Richard Trinity DeShed, one would think you're looking to be rescued from the worst possible torture with how slow you are pouring drinks tonight." Marilyn edged Ricky to the side with a bump of her hip. "Let me."

"Told ya," Ellen whispered through a giggle. "Hashtag couple goals."

"Do you want a drink?" Liam noticed the older couple had only prepared two glasses, presumably for themselves." Ellen shook her head, hair sliding across his arm. "Then let's be honest with ourselves and acknowledge that we're both tired. I think it's time for bed, darlin'."

"All in favor, say aye." Ellen was laughing as she raised a hand. "Aye."

"Aye," echoed from across the room, and Liam glanced up to see both Marilyn and Ricky smiling at them.

"Night, kids." Marilyn's smile widened. "Don't do anything I wouldn't do."

"Doesn't leave much." Ricky frowned. "Maybe don't listen to my ole lady."

"You're no fun." Marilyn grumped at Ricky and lifted her glass in a toast. "Seriously, though. To new beginnings."

"I'll drink to that." Ricky brought his glass to his mouth and made good on the statement. "See you in the morning, Irish, daughter-in-love."

"See you tomorrow. Wake me if LouCiel gets to you first." Ellen blew a kiss at the couple, and Ricky mimed catching it and plastering it over his heart. "Love you guys."

"Love you both," Marilyn shot back with a toss of her head. "Liam, too. You're basically family now. Rest easy, son."

Before he could recover from that, Ellen had them turned around and headed towards her bedroom.

"She meant that," he mused as he closed the door, already sliding his vest off to deal with it respectfully. "That's crazy."

"That's Marilyn." Ellen's smile turned fond. "She's honestly the best."

"She and Ricky both." Liam marveled.

Finding His Feet

Irish

Christmas Day dawned bright and cold, but he was warm and toasty in a comfortable bed with Ellen in his arms.

Staring through the curtains as the light strengthened, he thought back to the wealth of conversations he'd had yesterday. Ellen's words had struck a chord, plucked at his heartstrings with her confession of confident attraction. That had been reinforced throughout the day by talks with Ricky and Marilyn. Both had encouraged him to stay, offers of hospitality extended indefinitely.

Marilyn spoke eloquently about Ellen's heart and soul and how deeply she felt things. The undercurrent there was about strength and honesty, telling him without saying it that she wouldn't say she felt something if it wasn't there.

Ricky's discussion was more pragmatic and practical, talking about the club and fellowship he was building in his chapter of Legends. When Irish had asked about work opportunities, Ricky had laughed and informed him that Dolph had been looking for a partner for years.

Everything seemed custom crafted for him to stumble into this encounter.

When he shared his slight misgivings in general ways, Ricky had come closer, clapping a hand on Irish's shoulder.

"Finger of God. That's what my momma always called these kinds of things. Ultimate knowledge that there's a deep and powerful need, so the treatment is sought and redirected, bringing the two elements together. What happens after that is free will choices, but the confluence is divine intervention. He knew you needed someone after losing your brother, also saw Ellen's sorrow and LouCiel's giving heart looking for a stable influence—and brought you here. Simple as that." Ricky's fingers tightened harder. "What happens now is up to the two of you. I know what I hope for and understand how profound this is, the offer Ellen's made to you. Her love might be fast, but it's not casual. Next to Marilyn, she's the strongest person I know. I'm proud of her."

"Finger of God." Irish repeated Ricky's words with a nod. "That feels right, actually. I didn't understand it, but I had to ride up here to pay my respects. Had to be now. Had to be this highway. There were easier routes, but this was the only one that felt right." He blew out a hard breath. "Finger

of God brought me here. I told her last night that she was my karmic reward for being as good a person as I can be. Kismet. Finger of God. Two sides of the same coin, I think."

Ricky's fist thudded lightly against his other shoulder as the man released his hold and stepped back. "Karma or not, this is where I warn you that I know how to dispose of a body so it'll never be found. Wolves'll scatter bones across miles. You be good to my girls—my family—or you'll answer to me."

Recognizing the grief and love that drove the words, Irish brought Jerry's memory to the front of his mind as he crafted a response. With a steadying inhale, he said, "I'd never disrespect your son's wife and child in any way. He's not here anymore, and while I can't take his place, I can make sure that my space in their lives leaves plenty of room for remembering him. I don't think you'll have a reason to find a wolf pack, sir."

"No, I suppose I won't." Ricky's smile held an edge of pain. "That's good, Irish. Real good."

He wasn't aware Ellen had woken until she spoke. "Whatcha thinking about?"

"Good morning, darlin'. You're a sneaky waker. Took me by surprise."

"You didn't answer my question. I can feel your mind going a thousand miles an hour over there." She sighed and snuggled back into his hold, pressing them together even more. "Tell me."

"I still want to go to Bozeman before I head home to pack up. Seems disrespectful to come all this way and not finish the trip."

"What does Dolph say about the bike? When will it be ready?"

He was surprised by her questions but had answers readily enough. "Not for a couple of days. He didn't have a tire on hand, and everything's delayed because of the holidays."

"Then you spend Christmas with us, and we can drive up in my car tomorrow." Ellen wiggled and turned in his arms, facing him. "Unless you don't want to ride up in a cage."

Last night when they'd headed to her bedroom, they'd brought an unwelcome companion of anxiety with them. Ellen had been tense as they slipped between the sheets. In response, Irish had initiated a dating game old as the hills, asking endless questions about her likes and dislikes. Within fifteen minutes, she'd relaxed significantly, laughing softly at some of the queries, him chuckling at a few of the replies. Another thirty minutes passed before she'd fully unwound and twined her feet with his, locking them together in the middle of the bed, snuggled close as they could get.

So comfortable and content with the closeness and intimacy of the conversation, Irish hadn't been surprised when they'd both drifted off without sex entering the picture.

Her use of "we" just now told him a lot about Ellen's feelings, because she clearly saw herself as part of his path going forwards.

With a gentle caress of her shoulder, he composed an answer to her slimly camouflaged questions.

"Cage or bike doesn't matter for this leg of the trip. I did the bulk on the saddle. With the weather like it is, I don't think he'd begrudge me a few miles of comfort."

"Then it's settled. We head up there tomorrow. Day after Christmas sounds right."

"Easy as that?"

"Easy as that." She leaned closer and touched her forehead to his. "Marilyn won't mind keeping LouCiel for us, and the trip will bring you that needed closure."

Emotion flooded through him, and Irish tightened his arms, pulling her securely against him again, her face tucked against his neck. He fought for composure for a minute, steadying his breathing until he could talk through the feelings without choking.

"Us."

"What?" Ellen moved as if to slide backwards, but he kept his hold. "What is it, Liam?"

"Us. You said she'd keep Lucy for us." He swallowed hard. "I didn't understand how much it'd mean to me to be with you like this."

"If it bothers you—"

"No, not at all." He cut her off firmly. "This isn't me being bothered. This is me being overwhelmed with joy at how things are between us. Joy, and nothing less."

She bowed her neck, nestling her cheek against his chest. "I like that."

"MEMA!" Lucy's shout rattled the door, and he grinned at the slapping of her little feet as she sped up the hallway. "Is pwesents!"

"Should we head that way, join in on family time?" Irish pressed his lips to Ellen's temple. "I'd like that."

She melted in his arms, snuggling closer and he felt the brush of a kiss soft against his throat. "Family time."

Neither of them made any effort to move until Lucy's footsteps arrowed back to their bedroom door, and a tiny fist pounded hard.

Irish lifted his head and grinned at the door, calling, "Be right there, princess."

After the flurry of opening presents was over, breakfast went about as it had the previous day, and the rest of the time unspooled with cookies, laughter, and cocoa before bed.

Finally, the whirlwind of activity was over, and Ellen was pulling him down the hallway, smiling back at him over her shoulder, promises in her eyes.

Once the door was closed, he whirled, dragging her with him, and placed her back against the firm surface. He nudged the underside of her jaw with his nose and dragged his mouth along her neck, teeth and tongue working in tandem, lips caressing every inch of skin he encountered. Irish continued his exploration until she gripped his chin in her fingers, raising his head. Eyes blazing, pupils blown wide, Ellen said, "Bed."

"No argument from me." Lifting her against his chest, he walked the few feet to the bed and laid her back on the covers. "Just sayin', if you like any of these clothes, best lose them quick, darlin'."

His muttered demand in her ear set her in action, and within a minute, Ellen was stripped bare, stretched out in front of him.

Irish wasn't far behind her, kicking off his boxer briefs as he crawled up the length of the mattress to settle his weight on top of her.

"Want you," she whispered, fingertips twisting in his hair. "Want you, Liam."

"You got me." He slipped to one side as they kissed, tongues gliding in a sensuous dance, and reached a hand to the night table where he fumbled a condom from the stash he'd put there earlier. Eyes closed, he angled his head, deepening the kiss and swallowing down every sound wrung from her.

She took the condom from him and, true to her earlier demand, wasted no time preparing his cock. The fluttering sensation of her fingers along his length made his balls pull up, tingling spasms racking his muscles.

Rolling on his side to face her, he pulled her close and gripped her knee, dragging it over his hip as he thrust forwards. Sliding halfway in on a single movement, he held there for an instant, basking in the perfection of her hot channel holding tightly, pulling him deeper. Another push had the root of his cock grinding against her clit, and he cut off her cry of delight with his mouth, finding her kisses had turned desperate.

She pulled on his hip, wordlessly demanding he move, and he honored her request, unable to hold still. Ellen fucked him back, every glide and undulation setting off an answering reaction in her body until she gripped him harder, pulling her hips back as her muscles tightened. Hand on her breast, he tweaked and flicked her nipple, biting at her lips as he thrust into her over and over, each stroke feeling like it could be the last. Electricity bounced through his brain, whiting out his thoughts, and when he came, the orgasm took over, stuttering his hips through each pulsing throb of his cock. Ellen's rapid breaths carried half-spoken words comprised mostly of his name.

Out of breath and still shaking with the ferocity of his orgasm, Irish gathered her in his arms and rolled to his back, pulling her, so she covered him like his own personal blanket. Somehow, he managed to stay inside her, although he knew it was only a matter of time before he'd have to deal with the condom.

"Stay," he muttered when she would have moved. "Stay with me."

Ellen subsided, relaxing into him, head on his shoulder, knees on either side of his hips.

They remained like that for a few more minutes, then he groaned and reached between them, gripping the edges of the condom as he arched his back and slid out while she made a complaining noise. It took both hands to tie the damn thing off, and he tossed it towards the bathroom with a gruff, "I'll get it later."

Ellen's laughter was quiet and contented sounding as she shifted on top of him, adjusting to his change of position. "I'm not worried about it."

"Good." He yawned hugely, jaw cracking. "Darlin', you wore me out."

"Back atcha." Her yawn was more ladylike, halfway hidden behind her palm. "I could sleep right here."

"Then do." Irish pulled the covers over the both of them. "Door's locked, so Lucy'll have to knock in the morning if she doesn't head straight back to the new toys. We can sleep just like this without any issues."

"Okay."

***

Ellen

Sitting sideways in the passenger seat of her car, Ellen considered the man behind the wheel. When she'd shifted to this position, he'd tugged at her heels until she stretched her feet across his lap. Liam rested a hand on her ankles, fingers possessively curling around one. They'd talked through dozens of things in the past three days, and she had a good sense of who he was.

Wrapped up inside the attractive package was a loyal man. A good man who felt connections deeply. His affection for LouCiel was clear in every interaction, tolerance and kindness a hallmark. But there was still so much she didn't know.

It'll probably be a lifetime to learn him all.

The concept didn't scare her.

"Tell me more about Lyon." She broke the silence, only then realizing it had been comfortable and soothing. *Another good thing. He can be quiet without being mad.* "Anything at all."

"Oh, so many stories." Liam's tone was fond but carried a note of grief. "We went to Daytona one year and he tried to recreate a picture he'd seen online, standing on the saddle of his bike. Only he took it one farther and tried to do it in just his tighty-whities." He shook his head. "That did not end well for him. The leather of his boots slipped around on the seat so much the bike wobbled left and right like it was the drunk one instead of him. Crashed into a light pole and got a bad case of road rash on his ass. Then the bastard had to ride home the next day like that, crumpled fender and everything. Man cried and whined the whole way. Every time we stopped for fuel or food, the asshole was asking me to kiss it and make it better. We got back to the clubhouse, and he pulled his pants down to show everybody. Lyon had no shame."

Ellen was laughing halfway through the story, wiping her eyes by the end. "Sounds like the kind of guy Jerry would have gotten along with great."

"Would he have? That makes me happy."

"Oh, yeah. Jer was the life of the party. Always on, you know? At home he was different, would take the time to recharge." She wiggled deeper into the seat, adjusting the belt so it was more comfortable. "We were a good balance for each other."

"I'm glad he found you. Glad you had that with him."

"Me, too."

***

Irish

Boots respectfully to one side of the plot, Irish stood and stared down at the last remaining reminder of the man he'd considered closer than a brother. The granite stone was simple, just names and dates, with a small line of text underneath it all, which he assumed came with the design. Still, it resonated with him.

He was loved.

"I'm going to wander a bit. Give you some time, Liam. We're not in a rush."

Yanking his head up, he looked at Ellen, her gloved fingers squeezing his gently. Her expression was softened with sadness for him and his grief, and he loved that about her. Even without knowing Lyon, she felt the absence left behind because of his death. Irish nodded jerkily and tightened his fingers on hers before she slipped away.

He watched her for a moment, her head angled down as she read inscriptions on gravestones along the row. The mix of tall and short monuments stretched to the rise of the little hill they were on and beyond, one of the largest cemeteries in Bozeman. She was moving slowly, giving each grave the same attentive consideration.

Fuck, I love her.

Pulling his gaze from Ellen, he directed it back to the grave in front of him.

"Lyon, brother. Miss you every fuckin' day. Your bullshit and shenanigans. You kept me hopping. Wish I could have saved you, man. Follows me into my sleep, watching you die like that. Not ever gonna forget you. Couldn't, not when you helped make me the man I am." Irish sucked in a harsh breath, the back of his throat catching and choking him. He swallowed hard, forcing down the sounds threatening to break free.

"You see that woman here with me? Her name's Ellen. She's something else, man. Understands the brotherhood from the inside out. One of the best ones. Sexy, smart, and confident, and she's got this little girl, Lucy. Kid's a hoot, but such a good soul, just like her mother. I like her a lot, Lyon. You'd fight me for her, I know. I'd win, just so you know. I'll always win when it comes to her. I love her."

He glanced up again, finding Ellen now several rows away, but her gaze turned steadily on him. Irish gave her a chin lift that she returned with a little wave and wide smile. The wind threatened to lift one end of her scarf, and she tucked it inside her coat, hands rising to settle her hat on her head.

"If you were here, you'd demand some credit for all of this, I know."

Ellen was making her way towards him, and as she got closer, he could hear she was humming, the song light and melodic.

"And I'd tell you thank you, brother. Thank you for bringing me to the love of my life."

As she walked within touching distance, Irish reached for Ellen, wrapping his arms around her and pulling her tightly against him. He buried his face in the side of her neck, letting her scent and the feel of her in his arms pull him away from the edge of grief.

"You ready to go home, Karma?"

Trouble Brewing

Irish stood in Dolph's garage, the sharp tang of oil and rubber filling his nose as he ran a hand over Hester's freshly replaced tire. Dolph had come through, sourcing a new one despite the holiday slowdown. The bike gleamed under the shop's fluorescent lights, ready to roll again, but Irish wasn't in a hurry to leave. Not yet.

"Looks good, man," he said, glancing at Dolph, who was wiping his hands on a rag. "Appreciate you and your boys treating her right."

Dolph grunted, a faint smile tugging at his weathered face. "Ain't no trouble. Ricky'd have my head if I didn't. Plus, she's a beauty. You keep her maintained like this, she'll outlast us all."

Before Irish could respond, the shop door banged open, and Trashman strode in, his prospect cut slung carelessly over one shoulder. His eyes narrowed as they landed on Irish, a sneer curling his lip.

"Thought you'd be gone by now, outsider," Trashman said, voice dripping with venom. "Ain't you got a grave to cry over somewhere?"

Irish straightened, keeping his tone even. "Bike's just now ready. But I've decided I'll stick around a bit, see what Grass Creek's got to offer."

Trashman snorted, stepping closer as he thrust arms into his vest, his boots scuffing the concrete. "You already know what it's got ain't for you. Ellen's off-limits, you hear me. She's mine, always has been. You're just a fuckin' vulture circling a dead man's wife."

Dolph's head snapped up, his rag hitting the workbench with a soft thud. "That's enough, Nick. You don't talk to a guest like that, prospect or not."

Trashman ignored his father, jabbing a finger at Irish. "Legends don't need some east coast drifter sniffin' around. You don't belong here."

Irish met his gaze, steady and unyielding. "I'm not here to step on toes, Trashman. But I don't take kindly to being told where I belong. That's for me, and likely Ellen, to figure out."

Nick's face twisted, and for a moment, it looked like he'd swing. But Dolph stepped between them, his broad frame a wall. "Get outta here, Nick. Cool off before you do something stupid."

With a final glare, Nick stormed out, the door slamming behind him. Dolph sighed, rubbing the back of his neck. "Sorry about that. Boy's got a head full of rocks sometimes."

Irish shrugged, masking the tension coiling in his gut. "No harm done. Yet." But he knew better. Trashman wasn't the type to let it go.

***

Ellen

"He said what?"

She'd heard Liam correctly the first time, but couldn't believe her own ears.

He slid a calculating glance her way and shifted to lean casually against the kitchen door. Before he could respond, she kept going.

"No, don't tell me. I know that's exactly what Nick said. Dammit, the manchild never had a snowball's chance in hell, but get him to understand that without bloodshed is clearly a pipedream. God, why would he talk like that with his daddy in the room? Stupid and misogynistic are a lethal combination."

Crossing to the refrigerator, she pulled out two beers, passing one to Liam without comment.

"I think he's had an image of happiness in his mind. Gonna take something serious to push that out." Liam opened his beer and handed it to her, taking the unopened can from her hand. "Man's a fool."

Ellen took a deep breath and blew it out slowly. "I'm willing to confront him, if you think that'd help. It won't be comfortable, but I'd have you at my back, so I'm willing."

"Let me have another conversation with him. I'll get Ricky's advice beforehand, keeping him in the loop. I'm hoping to have him as my chapter president, so that will be good practice."

Sliding sideways along the countertop until she was next to Liam. "Smart man."

"Yeah? Gonna puff my chest if you keep giving me those kind of compliments." His arm settled around her shoulders, tugging her closer. "We're doing this together."

Ellen pressed her cheek to his chest, the smoothness of leather comforting.

"Yes we are."

The Breaking Point

Irish

The Legends MC clubhouse was a low-slung building on the edge of Grass Creek, its walls plastered with memorabilia — photos, patches, a dented fender from some long-ago wreck. Irish sat at a table with Ricky and Dolph, nursing a beer as the chatter of the club filled the room. Ellen was back at the house with Lucy, giving him a chance to feel out the Legends crew. They'd been welcoming, curious about his club back east, swapping stories of rallies and runs and finding friends in common. It felt good. Real goddamn good. Like a fit he hadn't expected.

The door crashed open, and Trashman stumbled in. His eyes locked on Irish, and the room quieted, tension rippling through the air.

"Well, look who's cozyin' up," Trashman slurred, weaving towards the table. He reeked of whiskey, and his face held a taint of desperation. "Think you can just waltz in here, take what's mine, huh?"

Ricky stood, his voice low and hard. "Nick, you're drunk. As president of the club you're looking to join, I'm giving you some good advice. Go sit down or get out."

"Fuck that." Trashman lurched forward, knocking over a chair. "This asshole's playin' house with Ellen, disrespectin' Jerry's memory. I'm the one who's been here. I've been waitin' for her. All this time. Me!"

Irish rose slowly, hands loose at his sides. "I'm not disrespectin' anyone, least of all Jerry. Ellen's a grown woman, makes her own choices. You don't get to claim her like some prize. From where I'm standing, she's made a clear decision, and you ain't it."

Trashman's fist flew, a wild swing Irish ducked easily. He grabbed the man's arm, twisting it behind his back and pinning him facedown on the table in one smooth motion. The prospect thrashed, cursing, but Irish held firm, voice calm. "We're done here, Trashman. You need to goddamn well cool it, or I'll cool it for you."

Ricky nodded approvingly as Irish released his hold and Dolph surged forward, hauled Nick up, and dragged him in a stumbling run towards the door. "Take him home, sober him up," Ricky ordered. "We'll deal with this later."

As the room settled, Ricky clapped Irish on the shoulder. "Handled that like a brother. You've got a cool head, Irish. That's somethin' we value around here."

Irish nodded, adrenaline still buzzing. "Just don't like seein' good people dragged through the mud." But he couldn't shake the feeling that Trashman's grudge was far from buried. Pushing that thought down, he hooked a foot around the leg of his chair and pulled it close. Turning it around, he settled with his arms crossed over the back of the chair. "Now, where were we?"

Laughter floated up from all sides and Irish forced his shoulders down, relaxing in tiny movements.

Ricky seated himself across from Irish and grinned. "I hadn't planned on bringing this up yet."

Irish lost every inch of relaxation he'd gained, tensing as he thought he understood where Ricky was taking the conversation.

"But, you're gonna anyway," called one of the members at a nearby table. "That girl is family to all of us, Ricky, go ahead with the inquisition. We're here for it."

Irish let humor show on his face, locking eyes with Ricky. "Go ahead, Prez, inquisition away."

"Why'd you join the military? Everything else we've covered makes sense. Everything except that one detail."

"I've talked about the brother I lost, the one buried in Bozeman." He paused and Ricky gave a brisk nod. "We actually grew up together, the push and pull of the neighborhood. You know how when you get to know someone inside and out, there's almost a sense you can read their mind?" Ricky nodded again. "Without talking about it, we separately joined the same branch only a couple of weeks apart. Laughed ourselves sick when we figured it out. We did basic together, got a tech assignment stateside for the first year, bunked together. Then we shipped out together. Me and Lyon. He always had my back, and I had his."

"That makes a hella lot of sense. Sometimes the government gets something right. Not often, and not for long, but sometimes." Ricky lifted his beer. "To Lyon. Ride in paradise, brother."

Tears threatened and Irish had to blink hard to drive them back. That simple acknowledgement of Lyon nearly broke him. He clinked his beer against Ricky's, and instead of falling apart, he echoed the sentiment, "Ride in paradise."

"Now," Ricky's eyes were glinting, smile lines gathered around the corners of his eyes. "What's your intentions with our Ellen? She's my daughter-in-love, always called her that and aways will."

"My intentions?" He looked around the room, noting how every eye was on him. Irish stood, pushing his chair to one side. "My intentions are long term. I'm here being vetted by a club chapter I'm hoping to one day join, because something about the area speaks to me. I plan on getting to know Ellen and Lucy as well as I can, because I want to fold my life into theirs. If they'll have me." He swept a glance around the room. "My intentions are long term."

"Good enough for me." Ricky leaned back in his chair and gestured to Irish's. "Cop a squat, brother. Can't have you standing when the rest of us are sittin'." He glanced over his shoulder, "Prospect, we need a couple new beers here."

Irish again settled on the chair and pulled in a deep breath.

Long term for sure.

***

Irish

Two days later Irish was tinkering with Hester in Ricky's garage, adjusting the chain tension, when the rumble of a bike cut through the quiet. It was so cold out that anyone with alternative transportation wouldn't be on their bike. That left him with just one person it could be.

He straightened, wiping his hands on a rag as, sure enough it was Trashman rolling up on a beat-up Harley, his face a mask of fury. The prospect killed the engine and dismounted, a crowbar dangling from one hand.

Fucking knew it wasn't done.

"Time's up, asshole," Trashman snarled, stepping closer. "You don't get to take what's mine. Not Ellen, not this town, not my fuckin' club. You don't get nothin'."

Irish squared his shoulders, dropping the rag. "Put that down, Trashman. You don't wanna do this."

"Fuck you." Trashman swung the crowbar, aiming for Irish's head. Instinct kicked in and Irish sidestepped, grabbing the off-balance Trashman's wrist and wrenching the weapon free. It clattered to the concrete as he shoved the man back, hard, sending him sprawling into a workbench. Tools crashed to the floor, and Trashman came up swinging, landing a glancing blow to Irish's jaw.

Pain flared, but Irish didn't hesitate. He tackled Trashman, pinning him to the ground, knee in his chest. "Now fuckin' stay down, goddammit. You're gonna get yourself hurt. I don't want that for you, man."

As Trashman writhed on the floor, the garage door flew open, and Ricky stormed in, Ellen and Marilyn on his heels. "What the hell's goin' on?" Ricky roared.

Trashman continued to thrash under Irish's hold. "He's stealin' everything, Prez! Ellen, the club. We al know that he don't belong! He's not from here."

Ellen stepped forward, voice trembling but firm. "Nick, stop it. I'm not yours—never was. Liam's here because I want him here. You don't get to decide that."

Irish relinquished Trashman to Ricky, who hauled the man up by the collar, shaking him back and forth like a rag doll. "You're done, prospect. This ain't how we do things. You've got one chance to walk away clean, and I'll need you to turn your vest in before the sun dips below the horizon, or I goddamned warn you that I'll strip that cut myself."

Trashman glared wordlessly, chest heaving, then spat on the floor and stumbled out, leaving silence in his wake.

Ellen slipped her hand into Irish's, squeezing tight. "You okay?"

He rubbed his jaw, grinning crookedly. "Yeah, darlin'. I'm good. Not even a scratch" But his eyes lingered on the door, wondering if Trashman's exit was the end… or just a pause.

***

Marilyn turned, gathering Ellen by the hand. "Let's start supper, give the boys time to get things straightened up out here." She glanced over her shoulder at Ricky. "Be ready to eat in about thirty minutes, honey."

"Yes, ma'am," Ricky gave her a sharp salute that made her laugh.

Ellen paused in the doorway and shook off Marilyn's hold. She whirled and ran back to Irish, her arms circling his neck as she buried her face against his chest. "You sure you're okay?" The words were muffled but Irish heard not just the question, but also the fear.

He tightened his hold on her waist, taking her weight as she leaned into the embrace. "I'm good, Ellen. Him and his skillset at, hell anything, are compromised by his belief that he doesn't have anything good in his life. Means his aim is for shit. I'm good." Irish turned his head and pressed a kiss against Ellen's cheek. "I'm good."

"Okay." Her affirmative response wasn't accompanied by any movement, so Irish kept holding her.

"Ricky, leave it for now. Come on in the kitchen and be my taste tester." She smiled at Irish. "You take care of our girl."

"Yes, ma'am," he used Ricky's cadence for the phrase and that got a laugh out of everyone. "Ricky, thank you."

"Don't know where that boy got so fucked up." Ricky shook his head as he followed Marilyn out of the garage.

The door clicked shut and silence settled on Irish and Ellen.

"I could hold you like this all night."

"I could be held all night." Her arms tightened around his waist. "This is nice."

"It is," he agreed. "That shit with Trashman wasn't nice. Wasn't fun at all. I hate he put Ricky in this position."

"You're going to make me talk about it, aren't you?" She sighed. "I got scared. We heard a big crash and then you were on the floor. Nick was there. I knew it wasn't anything good. Then your jaw was red, like you'd been hit."

"He got a tiny little blow in on me. Nothing to be worried about."

"Tell that to my heart. It's barely starting to unclench from the fear."

Irish gave her a squeeze. "Nothing to worry about, heart."

"You don't know Nick. He's a vengeful man. Always looking for someone to blame his own bad choices on. This is gonna kill Dolph. He loves that boy. That man. I know he's defended Nick's bullshit on the floor of the clubhouse more than once, urging a decision to keep his prospect vest."

"Dolph already knows what kind of man Trashman is. It shouldn't be a surprise to anyone. Prospect gets drunk, rides to the chapter's president's house, tries to put a beatdown on a welcomed visitor, then rides away, still absolutely soused, after being warned by the president he needed to turn in his vest." He shook his head, then bent to brush another kiss along Ellen's cheek. "We'll see what Dolph does, but I'm gonna bet on tough love. Kick him, force him to find his own path."

"Do you think he's done being a jerk about you and me?" Ellen leaned back, confident in his hold around her waist. "When Jerry was here Nick was never so direct. Jerry did warn me against being along with Nick. I didn't understand then, but I sure do now."

"I'm going to repeat Jerry's warning." Irish bent and captured her lips, keeping them both suspended in the absolutely brilliance of their burning attraction. "Do not ever allow yourself to be alone with that fuckwit."

"Promise," she whispered against his lips. She lifted to her toes chasing another kiss.

Of course he obliged her.

New Home, New Life

Irish

The clubhouse was packed, the air thick with cigarette smoke and laughter. Ricky stood at the head of the room, a gavel in hand, and called the meeting to order. Irish sat near the back with Ellen beside him, Lucy on his lap, her pigtails bouncing as she played with a toy car he'd fixed for her.

"Got some business," Ricky said, voice carrying. "First, Trashman's out. Behavior like the bullshit he's done don't fly in Legends. He's turned in his prospect cut and been told to stay clear. Any objections?"

A murmur of agreement rippled through the room, Dolph nodding solemnly. "Boy made his bed," he said. "I'll see he lies in it."

"Good." Ricky's gaze shifted to Irish. "Second thing. Liam Connor, our own singing Irish, need you to step up here."

"Not sure about the singing," he joked as, heart thudding, Irish handed Lucy to Ellen and walked forward, feeling every eye on him.

Ricky met him with a steady look. "You've shown us what you're made of, Irish. Cool head, strong heart, and a respect for what we're about. Legends could use a man like you. We're offerin' you a patch, full membership, if you'll have us."

Irish's throat tightened. He glanced back at Ellen, her smile bright and proud, then at the faces around him. Dolph, Marilyn, and all the brothers who'd welcomed him. "I'd be honored," he said, voice rough. "Liars & Fools was a touchstone after the military, but it's time to lay that down. I called last night and left the club. I'll hand over my cut when I go back to North Carolina to pack my stuff to move back here. This feels right. Grass Creek, Legends, all of it. It feels like home. All of this feels like I'm finally home."

Ricky grinned, handing him a Legends MC cut, the leather crisp and heavy with promise. "Welcome, brother."

The room erupted in cheers, fists pounding tables. Ellen stood, Lucy in her arms, and crossed to him, planting a kiss on his cheek. "Told you you'd fit," she whispered.

Irish slipped the cut on, the weight settling like it belonged. "Karma's good to me," he murmured, pulling her close, Lucy giggling between them. For the first time in a year, the hole Lyon left didn't ache quite so much. He'd found a new family. New family, new club, a new life and he'd damned if he'd let anyone take it from him.

End


~~~
~~~

THANK YOU

Thank you so much for reading *Outlaw Heartstrings*, book one in my Legends MC series.

ABOUT THE AUTHOR

Raised in the south, MariaLisa learned about the magic of books at an early age. Every summer, she would spend hours in the local library, devouring books of every genre. Self-described as a book-a-holic, she says "I've always loved to read, but then I discovered writing, and found I adored that, too. For reading...if nothing else is available, I've been known to read the back of the cereal box."

Also by MariaLisa deMora

Alace Sweets

A dark thriller, this book is not a light read. Filled with edge-of-your-seat suspense, this intense story commands the reader's attention as it drives towards the explosive ending. Alace Sweets is a vigilante serial killer, with everything that implies and is sure to trip all your triggers. Be ready.

At seventeen, Alace Sweets turned a corner in her life, taking the wrong shortcut home from school.

Resisting the harsh knowledge her attackers will never be made to pay for their actions, Alace takes a stand. Justice must be served, and if fate's scales are out of balance, she's determined to set things right as best she can.

When the laws of men fail, the rules of Alace prevail.

5-Star Reviews for Alace Sweets

"deMora has a superb story-line and exceptional character development. All of her

characters have such depth that will intrigue the reader..."
~Turning Another Page

"Hot, sweet, dark thriller."
~Beth D

"It will keep you on the edge of your seat and give you chills."
~Escape Reality Book Blog

"Disturbing, haunting, sickly; yet hot, sexy and heart racing!"
~Amanda L

"From the first page [deMora] pulls you into the world she has created and you do not even try to escape..."
~Little Shop of Readers Blog

"A must read for all those dark, gritty romance fans out there."
~Sweet & Spicy Reads

"You will find yourself so drawn into the story that the outside world is blocked out and your locking the doors and turning on all the lights."
~Danena F

"Don't judge me for bonding with a vigilante serial killer, she's more than what she does."
~iScream Books

"Thrilling...chilling...full of suspense, nail biting edge of your seat excitement."
~Tracey H

"Every time MariaLisa deMora picks up her pen (or opens her computer), she creates characters you want to believe in."
~Gail S

"Intriguing dark storyline, beautiful love story and nail-biting conclusion, what more could a reader ask for?"
~Manda M

"This book takes you a dark and twisted ride that is gripping..."
~Renee Entress' Blog

"This book is dark and gritty and I literally had to take a day off from reading it because it's that intense."
~My Girlfriend's Couch

"This is my favourite book so far from this author ... I recommend this book if you enjoy dark romantic thrillers."
~Cheekypee Reads and Reviews

"There's not enough stars to give this book and 5 just doesn't really do it justice!"
~DeLane C

"I couldn't put this book down from page one! Tried to stop & go to bed but couldn't sleep thinking about Alace and got up & finished the book."
~Debbie M

"MariaLisa DeMora, wordsmith that she is, made this a story of the enlightenment of a woman and finding love in a life where she has had none."
~Kat W

"Whatever deep dark trench [deMora] pulled a character like Alace from should be revisited again and often."
~Confessions of a Serial Reader

ADDITIONAL SERIES AND BOOKS

Please note that books in a series frequently feature characters from additional books within that series. If series books are read out of order, readers will twig to spoilers for the other books, so going back to read the skipped titles won't have the same angsty reveals.

Rebel Wayfarers MC series:

Mica, #1
A Sweet & Merry Christmas, #1.5
Slate, #2
Bear, #3
Jase, #4
Gunny, #5
Mason, #6
Hoss, #7
Harddrive Holidays, #7.5
Duck, #8
Biker Chick Campout, #8.5
Watcher, #9
A Kiss to Keep You, #9.25
Gun Totin' Annie, #9.5
Secret Santa, #9.75
Bones, #10
Gunny's Pups, #10.25
Never Settle, #10.5
Not Even A Mouse, #10.75
Fury, #11
Christmas Doings, #11.25

Gypsy's Lady, #11.5
Cassie, #12
Road Runner's Ride, #12.5

Occupy Yourself band series:

Born Into Trouble, #1
Grace In Motion, #2 (TBD)
What They Say, #3 (TBD)

Neither This, Nor That MC series:

This Is the Route Of Twisted Pain, #1
Treading the Traitor's Path: Out Bad, #2
Shelter My Heart, #3
Trapped by Fate on Reckless Roads, #4
Tarnished Lies and Dead Ends, #5

Rebel Wayfarers crossover stories:

Going Down Easy
No Man's Land
In Search of Solace
Puppy Love
Steel and Swagger

Mayhan Bucklers MC series:

Most Rikki-Tik, #1
Mad Minute, #2

Outlaw Heartstrings

Pucker Factor, #3
Boocoo Dinky Dau, #4

Borderline Freaks MC series:

Service and Sacrifice, #1
More Than Enough, #2
Lack of Inbetween, #3
See You in Valhalla, #4

Alace Sweets series:

Alace Sweets, #1
Seeking Worthy Pursuits, #2
Embarrassment of Monsters, #3
All the Broken Rules, #4

With My Whole Heart series:

With My Whole Heart, #1
Bet On Us, #2

If You Could Change One Thing:
Tangled Fates Stories

There Are Limits, #1
Rules Are Rules, #2
The Gray Zone, #3

Other Books:

Outlaw Heartstrings
Sidetracked Love
Only For You
Hard Focus
Salvaged Parts
Spark of the Lock
Dirty Bitches MC: Season 3

More information available at mldemora.com.